LOVE'S
REFINING
FIRE

LOVE'S REFINING FIRE

DOROTHEA ODOM

CITIOFBOOKS, INC.
3736 Eubank NE Suite A1
Albuquerque, NM 87111-3579
www.citiofbooks.com
Hotline: 1 (877) 389-2759
Fax: 1 (505) 930-7244

Ordering Information:
Quantity sales. Special discounts are available on quantity purchases by corporations, associations, and others. For details, contact the publisher at the address above.

Printed in the United States of America.

ISBN-13:   Softcover   979-8-89391-835-9
        eBook   979-8-89391-836-6

Library of Congress Control Number: 2025915393

TABLE OF CONTENTS

But He knows the way that I take.

When He has tested me, I shall come forth as gold.

(Job 23:10, NKJV, Holy Bible)

For You, O God, have tested us.

You have refined us as silver is refined.

(Psalm 66:10, NJKV, Holy Bible)

My highest regard to the US diplomatic community with which I was privileged to serve for over seventeen years.

My deepest gratitude to the Diplomatic Security Agents, the Marine Security Guard Detachments (*Semper fi!*), and the locally hired security forces of six host nations, including Colombia. You worked so diligently to keep us all safe. By the grace of God and those excellent security measures, I am here today. Thank you!

FOREWORD

<u>ove Under Fire</u>, published in 2024, is the abbreviated version of this present endeavor, <u>Love's Refining Fire</u>. This book affords a second look at the love story of Sheila Dunbar, a US Embassy office manager in Bogotá, Colombia, and Diego Santos, a Colombian physician.

This work is not merely a rehashing of the original story, but a revision and expansion of the text. The aim is a more in-depth look at the main and secondary characters, settings, circumstances, etc. for greater clarity.

The reader will notice a difference in the last names of Fabio and Diego, the father and son characters. This is not an error. It is deliberate. In Spanish-speaking countries, a person's last name is typically hyphenated and consists of both the father's last name and the mother's maiden last name. Thus, we have the father, Fabio Santos-López and his son, Diego Santos-Aragón. I have included some Spanish words and phrases to add authenticity to the text, as well as the rendition of what a Spanish speaker would say in English. (For example, a housekeeper named Alicia says, "Please to let me know…" instead of "Please let me know…").

The song lyrics in the closing pages of this book are my own – a nod to my enjoyment of Christian songwriting. Thank you in advance for your indulgence. May His name be glorified!

PREFACE

I arrived in Colombia in March 1985 and served in the Office of the Legal Attaché at the U.S. Embassy in Bogotá for three years. (Readers of <u>Love Under Fire</u> will note that the main character, Sheila Dunbar, was assigned to the embassy's Political Section. That does not change in this revised version under a new title.) During that era, direct-hire American employees of the embassy received, in addition to their regular salaries, extra pay of 15 percent for hardship and 25 percent for danger. We were required to ride in armored vans to and from work, followed by a *chase car* which served as a buffer between our vans and other vehicles. Pick-up times and routes were randomized (for purposes of security). Our US Government-leased living quarters met rigid security standards. Except for the Ambassador, most of us resided in apartments as houses were less safe (burglaries were common and numerous).

Buses were burned from time to time. Kidnappings for ransom, and assassinations of dissenters were common. Bombs exploded. In fact, one exploded at a bank a couple of blocks from my apartment, killing a woman walking past the bank. (Disregarding an embassy security directive not to ride buses, I had taken a bus to church that morning and returned to that same stop about an hour before the explosion.) I reported a nerve-racking personal encounter with an M-19 (April 19 Movement) taxi driver to the embassy's Regional Security Office. I was physically unscathed, but the incident compelled me to be more cautious going forward.

In this volatile atmosphere, I was among the staff who had to shelter in place (in my apartment) for four or five consecutive days because of threats from the terrorist element in Colombia. However, all was not doom and gloom. I found a wonderful church family at the Bogotá Baptist Chapel.

The places mentioned in this book are authentic: Kennedy City, El Chico Grande, Bogotá Baptist Chapel, National Park called *El Parque Nacional*, the Clínica Palermo, Tramonti's, and El Teatro Colón, all in Bogotá, as well as St. Ursula's Anglican Church in Bern, Switzerland, etc. With the exception of the terrorist Ivan Marino, the names of all persons, including the U.S. Ambassador at that time, are fictitious.

The car bomb explosion, mentioned in the prologue, really happened. Most notable among other true events were the storming of Colombia's Supreme Court by M-19 terrorists, the Nevado del Ruiz volcanic eruption in the town of Armero, and flooding at Chiva-Chiva. During M-19's takeover of the Palace of Justice, I monitored radio broadcasts and took notes for the Legal Attaché. Like Sheila, the character, I served for 48 hours on the embassy's Volcano Task Force. Although these true events influenced the narrative, I wish to inform the reader that <u>Love's Refining Fire</u> is not autobiographical.

INTRODUCTION

Narcotics – big business, big money. Colombian traffickers were infuriated by US efforts to eradicate the country's coca crop. They were even more incensed when Colombia signed an extradition treaty with the United States. (On June 25, 1987, the Colombian Supreme Court ruled the Colombian-US extradition treaty invalid.)

In April 1984, Colombian Minister of Justice Rodrigo Lara-Bonilla was assassinated on a side street in Bogotá. Threats to kill American diplomats ensued. The traffickers vowed that if such attempts failed, the diplomats' children would be targeted. Schools that those children attended became much more vigilant.

Of equal concern were the activities of groups like the Revolutionary Armed Forces of Colombia (FARC) and M-19, which funded many of their activities in cooperation with the narcotics traffickers often called *narcotraficantes*. The sale of drugs made possible more weapons purchases, more kidnappings for ransom, and more violence, including murders.

In November 1984, a car bomb exploded at the US Embassy's chancery in Bogotá. A deliveryman lost a leg. A woman passerby was killed by flying shrapnel.

Because of the bombing and the resultant security alerts, the US Department of State issued travel advisories to Americans planning trips to Colombia about off-limit areas and precautions to take. It also implemented a new policy for its diplomatic mission in Colombia: no minors at post. By late-January 1985, all the diplomats' children, most accompanied by their mothers, had been evacuated to the United States. Thus, there remained spouses without immediate families and a large contingency of singles, which increased each time the assignments of diplomats or support personnel ended at the mission. (The US Mission in Colombia consisted of the US Embassy in Bogotá; a consulate in Barranquilla; and cultural exchange centers in other major cities of the country, excluding Medellín, then the major operating base and headquarters of the drug-trafficking industry, as well as Calí in Valle del Cauca, where the Colombian Army's Third Brigade and revolutionary guerillas engaged in frequent combat.)

This story evolves at a time when Colombia's political crisis compelled then-President Belisario Betancur to declare the country under siege. Colombia's economic woes were of ever-increasing concern. High inflation and unemployment drove prices up and plunged the Colombian peso to an all-time low. Around the embassy, rumors circulated that a national strike was imminent.

This was a particularly violent era in Colombia's history, and the crisis was critical, threatening the very stability of the nation. Some believed that the worst would soon be over; others predicted that the worst was yet to come. Only time would tell. (Former M-19 member Gustavo Petro was elected as President of Colombia in June 2022 under the banner of Alianza Democrática M-19 formed in April 1990.)

oom! The blast of a car bomb shook the large, stone edifice with its imposing sign: Embassy of the United States of America. Two more thunderous explosions reverberated through leaping flames and dark smoke that filled the side street. Simultaneously, wrenching metal and shattering glass sailed upward into whirling debris, mingling with panic-filled screams and shouts as people ran for their lives.

Inside the embassy's Political Section, Sheila Dunbar fell to the floor – not from the force of the explosions, but from a fear that buckled her knees. Almost immediately, an announcement over the embassy's public address system brought the young, Black woman cautiously to her feet. Despite instructions to stay away from windows in case of another blast, she moved gingerly toward the one adjacent to her desk. Very slowly, she pushed the drape back a fraction of an inch and peered out.

Down in the streets, there was pandemonium. A Volkswagen Beetle was totally engulfed in a huge ball of fire. The blast had hurled its roof over the fence and onto the embassy's rear parking lot. Keening wails signaled the arrival of a firefighting crew and two ambulances. Curious office workers were leaning out of windows from various buildings across the avenue. An excited crowd began converging on an embassy guard squatting beside a prone figure.

Sheila thought, *My God! Those weren't empty threats. They've done it. They've really done it!* She suddenly felt clammy all over as she thought of Kevin, her five-year-old son. A frantic pounding began in her right temple and spread to her chest as she fumbled for the telephone. The staff of the off-site kindergarten assured her that Kevin was fine. With an enormous sigh of relief, Sheila sank onto a chair.

Her boss, Patrick Carmichael, walked into the office, his face pale and grim. To answer the question in her eyes, he said, "A woman's been hit in the neck, and some guy's leg is gone. Looks like they mean business."

CHAPTER 1

January 1985

Washington DC, Miami, Bogotá

Up until the moment Sheila Dunbar boarded the Eastern Airlines flight, everything was fine. Then, the nagging doubts began. No matter how often she told herself that she had made the right decision, the gnawing guilt persisted.

When the embassy's new policy of "no minors at post" was implemented, Sheila was offered the option to curtail her tour of duty and accept an assignment where her son Kevin could accompany her. Despite the dangers, the work was interesting and, she reasoned, she had another year left on her assignment; however, her mother was insistent that Kevin spend that year at home in Washington, DC. So, Sheila accompanied Kevin back to DC to be with her mother, returning to Bogotá to finish her tour of duty. How she would miss her son, although the extra benefits of post differential and danger pay would come in handy some day for his education. Still, her mother's words mingled with the shrill whine of the jet's engines as she disembarked, "For once in your life, think of Kevin!" Was she being selfish to leave her son with his grandmother instead of curtailing and choosing a safer assignment? Yet she knew the answer wasn't as simple as that. Her mother did not want Kevin to go anywhere overseas. Period.

Dorothy Dunbar had always been a shrewd and domineering woman, even when her husband was alive. In fact, Sheila's father used to tease her, "Dottie, you'd argue with a billboard." That, however, had never stopped her mother from arguing and, nine times out of ten, getting her way. In matters involving her grandson, she was relentless. She didn't approve of her daughter's career because it left Kevin "rootless." This latest incident, a bomb explosion at the U.S. Embassy in Bogotá, should have persuaded Sheila to take a Washington assignment or, better, get out of the Foreign Service altogether and transfer to Civil Service so she'd never have to work outside the US ever again. But, oh no! Sheila wouldn't "listen to reason." Her mother had branded her foolish for "traipsing back" to Colombia.

Dorothy still couldn't forgive Sheila for having taken Kevin to Dhaka, Bangladesh, her first assignment. She'd heard of the filth, the rats and snakes, and the pathetically few hospitals that served the teeming masses of that poverty-stricken nation. She'd warned Sheila not to take Kevin there, but she'd insisted on having her way. Well, Kevin had paid the price. When they returned to Washington, DC, her mother took one look at a thinner Kevin and launched into a tirade. He was "practically skin and bones", and she wasn't going to just sit back with folded arms and let Sheila finish him off! Sheila knew her mother was prone to exaggeration, but this barb hurt more than she cared to admit, even to herself. After all, neither she nor Kevin was emaciated. She had absolutely no regrets about her assignment in Bangladesh.

Sheila's self-control had been severely tested, but she stood her ground.

"Kevin is my son and my responsibility," she'd firmly stated. "Please trust me to know what's best for him."

"Best? Kevin won't have any stability until you stop roaming around like a gypsy."

At that, Sheila had lapsed into wounded silence. She'd thought of the Foreign Service Officer position, which she was eminently qualified for by brilliantly passing the exam and interview. Yet she had opted for the lower Office Management Specialist position so that she could devote more time to Kevin. Her mother obviously had overlooked that fact. After Bangladesh, she'd warned Sheila to take a Washington assignment or she would phone Robert. Sheila tried to explain that as part of her contract, she was obligated to serve worldwide unless grave illness or a crisis at post, necessitating evacuation, dictated otherwise.

Her mother's sole response was, "What about your obligation as a mother?" Again, her threat to phone Robert loomed over Sheila's conscience.

Sheila had endured three humiliating years of Robert Horne's affairs with other women before she divorced him. Dorothy insisted that Robert, being a top-notch attorney in the area, had provided her and Kevin with a good life – anything she wanted. Why complain about other women? He'd eventually settle down. When Sheila extolled the marvelous qualities of her father, Dorothy conceded that David *had* been a good man, one in a million, but he'd married late in life. He'd been forty when Sheila was born. So, he'd had plenty of time to "sow his wild oats." It was unfair to compare Robert with him.

Nevertheless, Sheila had gone through with the divorce and resumed her maiden name. Dorothy objected, "You should keep your married name for the sake of your child."

Sheila had been granted full custody of Kevin. Robert had been awarded visitation rights and ordered to pay child support. Immediately after the divorce, he remarried. He too opposed Sheila taking Kevin overseas, stating that visitation would be difficult, if not impossible. He would be entirely within his rights to file a petition to gain custody of Kevin. However, Sheila knew that flexing his legal muscle carried no real threat. He had rarely spent time with his little son prior to the divorce, preferring instead to substitute toys for a genuine bond. What was he trying to do – impress his new wife?

So, here she was back in Bogotá, feeling guilty over leaving Kevin behind. On the other hand, her widowed mother, adopted as an infant and bereft of a close bond even with in-laws, perhaps had been as lonely as she herself was now. In any case, the remaining twelve months of her assignment seemed to loom ahead endlessly.

CHAPTER 2

April 6, 1985

El Parque Nacional (National Park), Bogotá

A young man watched a woman from a distance, his attention riveted. She sat in the park alone, her head bowed as if totally absorbed in thought. The strap of her bag was loosely draped over one shoulder, her posture almost as still as a statue. Didn't she realize that beggars and muggers frequented this place? An attractive woman, unaware of her surroundings, could become an easy target here. From this distance, she looked too vulnerable to fend for herself. He sauntered closer to better observe her and was pleasantly jolted. She was beautiful! Short curly hair framed an oval face of flawless, rich mahogany that would be a pleasure to touch. Her full lips looked tenderly inviting. Her nose, with its slightly flared nostrils and inwardly curving bridge, was perfect. Sweeping long lashes concealed her eyes. If only he could see them!

Caramba! What insanity was this? In less than three months, he would be married; but here he was, drooling over some strange woman in the park! Yet the inner reprimand did not stop his eyes from sliding from her face to her slender neck and appreciating the delightfully curvaceous, trim figure in the tailored navy dress.

She looked up then. It startled him although she was not looking in his direction. Her attention was focused straight ahead. The lush grass, the dense range of trees, the bright flower beds, the marble statues, the splashing fountains, and the distant, hazy blue-green mountains were a most fitting frame for this magnificent specimen of womanhood; yet she seemed oblivious to her own attractiveness. He was not the only one admiring her, and therein lay the danger. Some of these scoundrels in the park could lure the birds from the trees with their flattery. He told himself that he was above such juvenile behavior. His singular concern was in forewarning her and, thus, protecting her from these wolves in sheep's clothing. At the same time, he wondered what her voice was like.

Jamming his hands into his pockets, he approached her.

"*Buenas tardes,*" he said in as grave a tone as he could muster.

She ignored him.

"*¿Usted es colombiana?*"

She didn't answer him or even spare him a glance. Was it possible that she was deaf? He sighed, ran unsteady fingers through his hair, and tried again.

"English?" he asked.

At last, she turned to look at him or, rather, right through him. He couldn't move. He was mesmerized by her eyes — lovely, dark orbs of some unknown distress. He should leave, but he couldn't. He stood there powerless, as irresistibly drawn to her as she clearly was repelled by him.

"*Bueno*, I suppose that puts me in my place," he responded lightly.

"I hope so," she said in a tone icy enough to freeze any man's spirit.

"*Bueno*," he repeated, feeling like a complete idiot and groping for words. "I – I am sorry if I am intruding. I want only to warn you –"

"Well, I'm warning *you*. Leave me alone."

Her tone was blade sharp. It did not match her eyes – her lovely, sad eyes. They fascinated him. *She* fascinated him.

"You have ten seconds before I scream for a cop," she announced, pointedly ignoring him again.

His heart sank. What could he do? Nothing except leave, but he would do so with his dignity intact. Without a backward glance, he marched off.

****

Turning, Sheila watched the man negotiate a grassy mound until his proud head and rigid, broad back disappeared from view.

It was then that she noticed the colorful blossoms bordering the walks. Her vision blurred. Impatiently, she wiped the tears away. This had to stop! The decision to come back to Bogotá had been hers and only hers. But how she missed her son!

Despondency swiftly descended upon her. The tears now flowed freely, and she didn't try to stop them. She soon realized that her lunch hour was almost over. She had to pull herself together and get back to the embassy.

Thank God, Kevin couldn't see her now. The rare sight of her crying would have upset him. He was twice as tender-hearted as he was mischievous.

She stood up, stretched, and headed back to work. She had needed a quiet place to harness her emotions. The National Park, situated on Carrera Séptima within a short walking distance of the embassy, had seemed ideal. Of course, she had been warned about the dangers of the park, but none of her colleagues needed to know that she had thrown caution aside this once. Besides, there was no printed policy to prohibit her from coming here, just a general tendency among the embassy staff to be extra cautious, especially since the car-bomb explosion. Well, this outing had done her a world of good. She was finally coming to grips with herself. She had to stop beating herself over the head. She would survive the remaining months of separation, and so would Kevin. Her only regret at the moment was wounding that poor man's ego. True, he deserved it for making a pest of himself, but nastiness had never been a part of her nature. He simply had been in the wrong place at the wrong time, a scapegoat for all her pent-up self-recriminations. If she could apologize she would. The thought almost made her laugh aloud. Apologize? That would have made the matter worse and given him the idea that she was being coy. He probably was already revamping his *machismo* by feeding his line to some other girl right now. Not that she was a girl. At twenty-one and fresh out of a women's college, she had been naïve and trusting. Then, she'd met Robert, a thirty-four-year-old partner in a prominent Washington, DC law firm. His looks and position had dazzled her; his smooth talk had swept her off her feet. Within a month, they were married. In love with love – that's what she'd been until Robert's infidelities had totally disillusioned her. Now, she was twenty-eight – almost twenty-nine – and, she hoped, a lot smarter. She wasn't bitter, but her failed marriage had taught her that genuine love fostered respect. In any case, marriage was no longer of any interest to her. Her first priority was getting through this assignment safe and sound so she could return to DC and Kevin. She'd phone him tonight; hearing his voice was always a tonic. A call would also appease her mother – for the time being.

Her wristwatch indicated that she had only five minutes to get back to work. She looked up into a cloudless sky, and her mood lightened. Quickening her pace, she left the park behind.

The next day, the embassy's Regional Security Office issued a new policy which stated that all employees, American and non-American, would be restricted to the embassy chancery during the lunch hour until further notice.

CHAPTER 3

From his bedroom, Diego Alejandro Santos-Aragón stood staring through a wall of glass, yet not really seeing the canopy of countless twinkling city lights.

It had been eight days since his encounter in the park. Piqued pride had kept him away over the next two days, but he'd been back there during his lunch break every day since – to no avail.

Was she staying away to avoid him? Not that he would blame her, but that didn't stop him from wanting her to be there. Was she a tourist, or did she live in Bogotá? Would he ever see her again?

This made no sense! No matter how often he tried to supplant the image of her with thoughts of his fiancée, he could not. He was fond of Rosa, but the sight of her had never affected him like this.

He was a physician. His work was immensely gratifying. His days and almost all his evenings were full, either with work or social events. The only thing he lacked, his father had informed him, was a wife. True. He was thirty-one. All his friends and associates were married. Most of them had children. Of course, he'd never felt the need to rush into matrimony, but he was a virile man and didn't relish the idea of becoming an eccentric old bachelor wed only to his profession. He wanted a home with a loving woman, someone he could share his innermost thoughts with. He also wanted children. And if his wife also had a fulfilling career, perhaps she would empathize with the demands of his medical practice. Well, his fiancée had made it clear that she had no intention of working. Why should she? She was the daughter of an immensely wealthy man. Everything had been hers simply for the taking. She did want children, she'd said, but not for a long time. That was fine with him. After all, she was only twenty-two and would need time to adjust to married life first.

He kept picturing Rosa as he had seen her only two nights ago at his sister's birthday party. Her doll-like prettiness would turn any man's head, yet he did not love her. In fact, by the time they met, he had begun to wonder if love existed except in novels and movies. When his parents invited the Galáns to dinner, and they'd brought their daughter with them, he'd suspected matchmaking; but he hadn't been averse to playing along. Now, he realized that he should not have. Marriage was not a game.

Why the soul searching now? He'd certainly known, or at least suspected, all this before he'd presented Rosa with the engagement ring. It hadn't seemed so important then, and he'd voiced no objection when their parents suggested a four-month engagement. He'd also known how much the marriage would mean to them. His father needed financial backing to expand his textile operations. Sancho Galán-Garza wanted the social prestige attached to the Santos name. The announcement of the engagement appeared in the major newspapers and magazines some weeks ago. He would cause both their families a great deal of embarrassment if he backed out now. But was not embarrassment better than a lifetime of regret?

Then, there was the matter of his faith. When he'd stated that Jesus Christ was the Lord of his life, Rosa had looked upon him with pitying eyes and hinted that he'd get over it. She believed in the tenets of the Catholic faith, but she saw no reason to go overboard with religious talk of being *saved*. "Saved from sin?" she jeered. She was a good person, and that was enough, she'd firmly stated.

He heaved a gigantic sigh. He could not risk tying himself to Rosa. Underneath that sweetness and charm was a Christian in name only, a spoiled child accustomed to always getting what she wanted and capable of some rather dramatic tantrums when she did not. Eventually, he realized that her sole interest in him hinged on her gaining a higher-class status in Colombian society. And what had he hoped to gain by marrying her? A pretty wife to grace his home and bear children, but initially to please his parents, especially his father. He was not entirely without fault. And, in all honesty, he too had his shortcomings – his tendency, for example, to become overly absorbed in his work. Rosa's need for attention definitely would not tolerate that.

Diego concluded that it would not be fair to marry Rosa while another woman's sad, lovely eyes haunted him day and night. Besides, she might not be any more a Christian than Rosa. If she was not, did it matter if he never saw her again? Yet he couldn't get that woman out of his mind. God knows he had tried! Well, he would have to; it was the only way he could deal with the reality of his present dilemma. He was behaving like a lovesick teenager, not like a man.

Man – the word echoed mockingly through his head. After his medical studies and residency in the United States, he returned to Colombia, moving back under his father's roof and his thumb. But in his decision not to marry Rosa, he must stand firm. His father would have to look for financial backing elsewhere. He surely would be able to obtain a business loan. He must be made to see Diego's point of view. Brave words, but how? He didn't want to hurt his father. Should he break the news gradually? No, there was not enough time for the subtle approach. He must be forthright and honest.

He whirled away from the window and began pacing the floor, finally dropping onto a stuffed chair. Rehearsing an opening argument did nothing to restore his self-confidence. He walked back to the glass wall. He was mentally exhausted and apprehensive of challenging his father's authority. He, a grown man of thirty-one, dreaded confronting his own father about the most important decision he would ever make – correction: *had* made.

He thrust a hand through his thick dark hair, as was his habit when he was upset. Once again, the vision of the woman in the park tangled his senses. What was wrong with him? She was like a poison that had spread too rapidly through his system to be expunged! It was a good thing that she had threatened to summon the police before he'd made a complete jackass of himself. Actually, she had used the word *cop*, an Americanism. Was she from the United States? He supposed he would never know. He had done the only thing he could do: leave with his pride intact. And what good was pride, when he yearned for so much more? He wanted *her*! He stood there staring at the tiny lights of the sprawling metropolis, wondering where she was, hoping against hope that he would someday find her again and perhaps be given a second chance. Absurd! Still, the vision of her lingered clearer than ever in his mind's eye. He knelt to pray, but no words would come.

14

ownstairs, the rest of the family was having dinner.
"Diego hardly touched his plate tonight. Something is troubling him," said Carmenza, Diego's stepmother. She was a short, plump woman; her professionally tinted brown hair did little to soften the lines of her face. His mother had died of breast cancer when he was a boy of ten.

Her husband, Fabio, was a distinguished-looking tall businessman with salt-and-pepper hair and a well-trimmed mustache.

"Nothing that I cannot make right, *querida*," he said with a reassuring pat on her hand.

Carmenza continued to frown. "You do not think he is still grieving the loss of that child?"

"No, no, it is not that. For a doctor, Diego is a bit too softhearted, but the accident happened over a year ago. Since then, he has accepted that he could have done nothing more to save the boy. The stallion had battered his head, and the bleeding —"

"*Papi,* please!" Conchita said with a grimace. She was a pretty girl of fifteen, the youngest of the Santos siblings, with dimpled cheeks and winsome eyes that seemed too large for her face.

"Sorry, *chica*," he said.

"If you're going to be a doctor, you'll have to stop being so squeamish," seventeen-year-old Carlos told his sister.

"A doctor?" Fabio asked with raised brows.

"Yes, like Diego," Conchita replied.

"You're too fainthearted," persisted Carlos. "Better for you to be a doctor's wife."

"Leave her alone, son. There is plenty of time for your sister to decide whom she will marry," Fabio said, deliberately evading the issue of his daughter's aspirations. He was of the old school and believed that a woman's place was in the home, not the workplace.

"But not for our big brother, *cierto*?" the roguishly handsome José remarked with a sly wink. He was twenty-five and was always quick to offer his opinion.

"That has already been decided *and* announced, as you well know, José. Rosa will be the perfect wife for Diego," Carmenza said, a look of great contentment on her face.

"But will *he* be the perfect husband for *her*?" José asked, ravenously chomping his steak. There was a reproving look on his father's face, but if José noticed, he chose to ignore it. "Sometimes I think Diego hasn't the wit of a braying donkey."

"José, that will be enough," his father growled.

"No, Fabio. Please allow him to speak. I want to know what he means by this insult to Diego," Carmenza said, turning to José.

"I mean, *Mamita*, that Diego does not behave like an engaged man. Does he woo Rosa? No. He is too busy with his precious patients and prescriptions. Now, if *I* had such a fiancée —"

"But you do not," his father broke in. "You just concentrate on the family business, and some day, your turn will come. In the meantime, keep your nose out of your brother's affairs."

"Well, I do not think he really wants to marry Rosa," Conchita commented.

Fabio blinked as if the very idea were blasphemous.

"Of course, he wants to marry her. Otherwise, why would he have proposed to her?" Carmenza asked.

"Maybe because she's so pretty, but as Teacher Garzón always says, 'Beauty is as beauty does.'"

"Must you always quote the worn clichés of that four-eyed, cow-faced old maid?" Carlos drawled.

"Just because she wears glasses is no reason for you to bad-mouth her!" Conchita huffed.

"I'm not bad-mouthing *her*. I'm bad-mouthing *you*!" he retorted.

Conchita's eyes blazed. "Why, you skinny, pimple-faced —"

"*Hijos, hijos!*" Fabio bellowed. "There will be order at this table or absence from it. Is that clear? Carlos?"

"*Sí*," Carlos muttered, clamping his jaw down on his anger.

"Conchita?" he inquired as she sat in reticent silence.

"Concepción," he intoned ominously. He only called her Concepción when he was displeased.

She answered with gentle defiance. "All I was trying to say when that — when Carlos butted in is that maybe Diego's happiness does not lie with Rosa. Maybe —"

"Maybe your mouth is bigger than your brain, *muchacha*. Have you not yet learned that obedience is better than *defiance*?"

Now, it was Carmenza's turn to blink. He had missed the mark on this one, substituting defiance for what should have been *sacrifice*. However, she was not going to correct him, especially in his present mood.

"Such impudence," Fabio went on, "will not be tolerated."

But, *Papi*, if only you'd listen to what I have to say —"

"You have nothing more to say!" Fabio roared. "Go to your room, Concepción. Now!"

Conchita meekly gave in, but once she was upstairs and out of earshot, Carmenza gently asked her husband, "Was it necessary to be so hard on her, Fabio?"

"Forgive me, *querida,* but I had to show her who is master of this house!"

José and Carlos exchanged knowing glances, then let out a couple of snickers and conspicuous throat clearings.

Fabio didn't verbally respond to them but undoubtedly disapproved of what he considered their disrespect. For right after patting his wife's hand, he scowled and tackled his steak with a ferocious clatter of knife and fork, which effectively forbade anyone to utter another word.

CHAPTER 5

Fabio Alonzo Santos-López had a secret. His business was on the brink of bankruptcy. The market of thirty years ago, when he had taken over the business from his father, had expanded. Competition over the last five years had been steadily increasing. He had been warned by his financial advisors to diversify, but at the time the business was bringing in pesos hand over fist. Yet even when he realized that profits were decreasing, he ignored the warning signs. He had neither the acumen nor the desire to become involved in other enterprises. Textiles had been his family's lifeblood for the last four generations.

His frequent show of arrogance stemmed from the knowledge that his was a highly venerated and respected ancestry. The Santos lineage dated back to the Spanish nobles who had settled in Nueva Granada, as Colombia was once known, in the late 1500s. One Santos had even been associated with Simon Bolívar, the Great Liberator himself.

Fabio told himself that he had it all: honor, wealth, and the affection and devotion of a lovely wife, three sons, and a daughter. Yes, he had it all – that is until he learned of the dire state of his finances some months ago. Well, soon, he would have more money than he could spend. Sancho Galán-Garza would be his salvation. Starting as a small-time farmer, Galán eventually diversified his holdings; expanded his coffee-exporting business internationally; and was now one of the richest men in Colombia. His coffee plantation in Antioquia Province's Aburrá Valley was such a huge success that he had recently sold it and relocated to Bogotá, where he was in search of new investments and a higher social status. Galán needed Santos's connections, and Santos needed Galán's money. So, when Fabio Santos engineered the engagement of his oldest son to Sancho Galán's only offspring, it was a happy day for both families.

The wedding was scheduled for the last Saturday in June, six weeks away. Fabio told himself that nothing could go wrong now. Yet he couldn't stop thinking about the dinner conversation last night. It came to mind as he sat, hard at work in his book-lined study at a massive desk of burnished mahogany, surrounded by rich leather furnishings and brass light fixtures.

Carmenza tended to obsess over little things. And Conchita? She was only a child. What did she really know of the matter? Yet her words kept buzzing through his head like an annoying fly. This was asinine! He was worrying needlessly. Diego *would* marry Rosa. He had always been a good son, complying with his father's wishes. Well, except in two instances, and those had proven to be of minor consequence in the long term. As a teenager, Diego had announced that he wanted to attend church services in Kennedy City, a neighborhood seldom frequented by the elite of Bogotá society. Fabio had been tempted to whip some sense into the boy and would have, but Carmenza had intervened. It was a phase Diego was going through, like all other teenagers, she'd said. Finally, he'd given in to her and permitted Diego to frequent that *barrio's* nondenominational church, if such could be called a church. Until he'd left to study medicine in the United States, he had attended services there. He still did, but he also accompanied the family to the Catholic mass twice a month. Gradually, Fabio concluded, his son was coming around to sound thinking. The second instance involved Diego's decision to become a doctor. Naturally, he'd wanted Diego to follow in his footsteps, but medicine was a respected profession. He could not have made a better second choice himself. And besides, he had two other sons, one of whom was bound to embrace the family business – and did. He was proud of how diligently José was applying himself. (Now, if only he could tame that tendency to be so opinionated.) Well, he had indulged Diego, although he'd definitely held the upper hand. Had Diego chosen a career of which he disapproved, he simply would have refused to finance his education. Anyhow, they had never had a serious clash of wills and never would. Diego had left that rebellious streak behind with his teen years. His serenity restored, Fabio returned to the work at hand with vigor. It was five after nine that night when someone knocked on the door.

"Enter!" he called out.

Looking up, he broke into a smile as Diego walked in. Of medium height with a broad, muscular chest and narrow hips, the young man looked more like an athlete than the typical physician. He was tan and handsome, possessing the kind of bearing and impeccable manners that would win any girl, his father mentally noted with pride. The Galáns certainly weren't getting the short end of the stick.

"Have a seat, son," he said, motioning him to a nearby chair and offering, "Sherry? Brandy?"

"No, thank you, *Papá,*" Diego said, taking a seat.

Noticing his son's hesitation and pushing aside his own mounting uneasiness, he teased, "Well, what is it? Have you had a spat with Rosa?"

"No, nothing like that. It's –" Diego broke off.

"Out with it. I don't bite, you know," Fabio said with casual humor.

Diego let out a deep sigh.

"*Papá,* there is no easy way to tell you this. I've been thinking about the engagement –"

"So have I. You have been working too hard. Instead of a two-week honeymoon, why not take a month?"

"*Papá,* I don't want –"

"Don't want it? What's the matter? Not man enough to keep the old pump at full pressure that long?" He let out a crude chuckle that incensed his son.

"For God's sake, will you listen to me? I'm not going to marry Rosa!"

The older man was stunned but seemed to recover remarkably. There was nothing in his voice of the shock he was feeling when he responded. "You seemed willing enough before. What has changed your mind?"

"I realize," Diego said with an unsettling calmness, "that Rosa and I are not suited to each other."

"Just like that? Overnight?"

"Not overnight. Almost from the beginning, but I was reluctant to displease you."

"Now you are totally indifferent to my displeasure," Fabio icily commented.

"Certainly not. I assure you –"

"There is only one way to assure me. Marry her."

"I can't! It would be a mistake."

"Rosa is young and beautiful."

"I don't love her!" Diego exclaimed, leaping to his feet.

"Sit down, Diego," Fabio sternly ordered. Diego subsided into his chair, his entire demeanor one of suppressed agitation. "That's better. I don't know what has come over you. I have never known you to be impulsive."

"I'm not impulsive. I told you. I don't –"

"I know, I know. You don't love her," his father said in the tone of one humoring a small boy. "But that will come with time, my boy – after the marriage. And if it doesn't, well, there are plenty of other women. Surely, you'll find … love with one of them."

This last was spoken with a touch of derision, and Diego steeled himself to remain calm. "*Papá*, you're talking as if this whole thing is some kind of game. Women aren't toys. I wouldn't want to hurt the woman I marry."

"Of course, you wouldn't," his father said in a soothing tone. "What she knows nothing of cannot hurt her. A good husband plays by the rules. Rule number one: discretion," Fabio said with a wink, then more soberly, "I never hurt your mother, and I have never hurt Carmenza."

"You'll excuse me if I keep my seat and hold my applause," Diego dryly remarked.

Fabio slammed his fist down on the desk in fury. "*Maldito!* You will not use that tone with me. I am your father. I do not have to justify myself to you!"

"And I am a man, *Papá*. Must I justify myself to you?"

"There can be no justification where you are concerned."

"There is another very important reason why I can't marry her."

"Important, you say. Well?"

"She is not a believer, *Papá*."

His tone was solemn, which his father found quite amusing. He burst out in hearty laughter. "You are joking, no? Believer – as in *Jesus fanatic*?"

"As in born again," Diego firmly declared.

"Diego, Diego, don't look now, but your halo is losing its luster. You haven't always been a saint, you know."

"I know that. Jesus came to call sinners to repentance, not the righteous."

"It seems that the Catholic faith you were raised in is no longer good enough for you," Fabio concluded, then asked, "So, what are you now – a preaching physician?"

"You do not understand."

"It is *you* who do not understand. Too much is riding on this marriage for you to back out now, Diego."

"I think Galán needs you more than you need him."

"I will be the judge of that. You just keep your part of the bargain."

"I can't."

"Think of the disgrace, Diego. Do you want that?"

"Of course not."

"Then –"

"I'm sorry."

"Sorry? You're not sorry. Not for one moment do I accept that flimsy *believer* nonsense. Do you know what *I* think? I think you're already sneaking around, and now you fancy yourself in love," Fabio sneered.

"If you'll excuse me." Diego stood up and headed for the door.

"I am not finished with you yet," Fabio growled, following him out the door. He grabbed Diego's arm as he turned to go up the staircase.

"How dare you turn your back on me!" he hissed.

Diego faced his father squarely. "I am no longer a child. I refuse to be treated like one."

"Then stop behaving like one. You have an obligation to your family, and you will fulfill it!"

"Regardless of my personal feelings?"

"So, it has come down to that. Emotions are fickle, Diego. Are you so selfish that you would trade your family's honor for some three-night tryst?"

"It's not like that!" Diego snapped, raking a hand through his hair.

"I don't *care* what it's like," Fabio gritted through clenched teeth. "You are going to listen to me. Most men would sell their souls for a girl like Rosa."

"Then, let one of *them* marry her."

"One of them did not propose to her. *You* did!"

In frustration, Diego closed his eyes for an instant, then slowly enunciated in order to drive home his point. "*Papá*, the world will not collapse if I break my engagement to Rosa."

"*Your* world will. You will find yourself without credentials, basically out of the medical profession here."

"My work stands on its own merit."

"Merit?" Fabio scoffed. "There isn't an administrator in this city who can't be bought."

Diego threw up his chin, his eyes narrowing. "There are many towns and villages in need of doctors."

Fabio was shaking his head. "Diego, you are delusional! How long do you think you would last, away from what you have known all of your life? Probably a year at most."

"We will see, *Papá*. We will see," Diego countered.

He continued up the stairs, bone-weary and ready for a solid night's sleep. He half expected further protest from his father, but there was none. As he reached the top of the stairs, a low moan caused him to turn and look down. The sight of his father slumped over the banister and clutching his chest sent him vaulting back to the foot of the stairs.

CHAPTER 6

Sheila locked her file cabinets, rechecked them to be sure that no classified materials had been left out, and called, "Good night, Pat!"

"Night, Sheila!"

She reached the door and stopped. "Will you and Liz be able to make it on Sunday?"

"You bet."

"Great! See you then."

It was almost six o'clock. The grocery store would close at nine. Wanting to avoid the Saturday morning crowds, she'd decided to shop tonight for her buffet on Sunday. She hurried downstairs to catch one of the armored vans. While her fellow passengers made light conversation, she leaned back and reflected on her time in Bogotá. She considered herself fortunate to be managing the Political Section under Patrick Carmichael's supervision. He was demanding but fair and always quick to compliment her on a job well done, unlike the supervisor at her previous post in Dhaka. Well, that was the advantage of being in the Foreign Service Corps. Like the weather, the staff changed with each new assignment. If you had a bad break at one post, the next one, more than likely, would have a better work environment. Despite the dangers, the loneliness without Kevin, and her large but often drafty apartment, she was enjoying this assignment.

This had been a good week. Pat had attended the embassy's Country Team meeting, usually chaired by the Ambassador, on Monday with little enthusiasm. However, he returned with the good news that starting next Monday, employees would be allowed outside embassy grounds at lunchtime, although they had to remain within specified parameters. Secondly, the Chargé d'Affaires (temporary head of the embassy) was being transferred to Stockholm and, upon his departure, would be replaced by a new Deputy Chief of Mission (DCM). The past few months hadn't been easy on Mr. Brighton as the strain of doing double duty had brought on tremendous stress, which he had not handled well. His blow-ups were the talk of the staff. As for newly arrived Ambassador Rick Váldez, he was a veteran of several "hardship" posts and had a reputation for running a "tight but smooth-sailing ship."

The van finally stopped at Sheila's apartment building, a red brick skyscraper in the northern sector of the city called El Chico Grande. It stood amid colorful vegetation and an emerald-green lawn across from a public park. She stepped down and was accompanied to the lobby by an armed escort from the chase car. The doorman, dressed in a burgundy uniform trimmed in black braid, admitted her with a respectful nod and a pleasant, *"A sus órdenes, su merced"* in response to her thanking him for summoning the elevator. He always executed his duties with deference, but ever since she had generously tipped him for a carrying a heavy box from the van into the elevator for her, he had been exceptionally attentive.

Although the old-fashioned "At your service, Your Grace" sounded a little over the top to her, she had no doubt that the young man was earnest. He nodded again and lifted his cap as she stepped into the elevator. She suppressed her amusement until the door clicked shut, and she was gliding up to her ninth-floor apartment. There is a great gulf between the social classes in Colombia. Sheila supposed that accounted for such mannerisms. It was a novel but not unpleasant experience in this city of some six million people.

She quickly changed into a dark-green jogging suit and white sneakers, took the elevator down to the garage, and drove to the grocery store. Her twice-a-week cleaning lady was to have done the shopping, but she called yesterday to say that her grandfather had died, and she would not be able to come tomorrow or be available for the Sunday buffet. The whole family would be attending the funeral, so there was no chance of getting either her younger sister or cousin to replace her. Engaging someone else on such short notice would be difficult, if not impossible. So, she would just have to do the best she could on her own. But would her best be good enough? If only she hadn't invited thirty people!

Judging by the few social events she'd attended, the guests would expect liquor to be served. Apart from her preference for an occasional glass of wine, there was no excuse for not meeting that expectation, but she would skip the hard stuff and prepare a red wine-based sangria, besides having plenty of "mocktails" and sodas on hand. It was assumed that everyone would drink to be sociable. Why the assumption? At this point, hers was "not to reason why" but to get through the event itself, which she was hosting only in the spirit of reciprocation.

The *Carulla* that she patronized was one in a chain of supermarkets. It was also one of the better-stocked stores with a wide variety of products. Sheila found every item on her list, although shopping for thirty people was no easy task. But then, neither was resisting the temptation to buy every tropical fruit on display. As she wheeled her large cart to the checkout cashier, she noticed that all the women in the supermarket were wearing high heels, even those in jeans. *So, I'm a slob,* she told herself with a shrug. At least she was comfortable. No cramped toes or aching feet. However, the combination of a nine-hour workday and the shopping left her physically drained. She was glad to get to her apartment and a warm bubble bath. After a steaming cup of lemon tea and a simple tuna, lettuce and tomato salad, followed by her usual regimen for skin and teeth, she was ready for bed. As her head touched the pillow, she sent up a fervent prayer of thanks that new dangers had been kept at bay since she'd arrived back in Bogotá. Memories of Kevin's hilarious antics filled her mind as she drifted off to sleep.

CHAPTER 7

Sheila got up early that Saturday morning. She exercised, showered, and went for the wines, sodas, and ingredients for mocktails, arriving back at her apartment by eleven o'clock. If she prepped everything this evening, she would be able to attend Sunday morning services and get back to her apartment in time to be ready for her afternoon guests.

When she'd first arrived in Colombia, she doubted that she'd find a congregation that was as welcoming and grounded in the Bible as her home church back in Washington, DC. At the Bogotá Baptist Chapel, she'd found both and was truly thankful. The diverse membership of Americans, Canadians, Colombians and several other nationalities turned out to be a bonus. While many of her colleagues chose to socialize only with other Americans, she interacted with the local populace outside of those at the embassy, forming a few new friendships along the way and broadening her cultural experience. She herself had a fear of firearms, but it was rather reassuring to know that certain church members were armed.

She quietly hummed "In the Garden" as she proceeded to her balcony to check her only plant, a giant yucca, but spared it no more than a glance before gazing off into the distance. The view today was gorgeous! It was also unusual as the city of Bogotá had been shrouded in a grey haze of drizzling rain for the last two weeks. Looking at the pristine white clouds in a bright sky, she knew she couldn't stay inside all day. Today was a day to savor the sights and sounds of nature, even in a city as humongous as Bogotá. She would go out, just for a little while, and prepare for the buffet later.

And that's how she found herself in her little black MG headed for National Park two days before some restrictions were to be lifted for embassy staff. She was actually there, shoving her clutch purse into her interior jacket pocket and locking her car doors, when the reality of her surroundings registered in her brain. Why had she come back here? She didn't know why except that this was a very nice park, and she had missed it. She could only hope that no one from the embassy saw her. Meanwhile, it was silly to just stand here. Yet halfway across the park, her stomach knotted. Suppose *he* was here? *Stop it! You're getting paranoid.* So, she took a leisurely stroll in the park, finally choosing a bench far from where she had sat before. It seemed fitting because this time was different. She was no longer brooding. Kevin was just a phone call away, and the remaining months no longer seemed to be dragging by.

It had rained last night, washing the air clean and drenching the ground. Sheila inhaled the scents of rich, moist earth, marigolds, and roses. It was good to be here, good to be alive.

****

At that moment, Diego was walking through the park. He was thinking about his father. The surgery had been successful, but the convalescence was going slowly. Diego couldn't shake off the conviction that he was to blame. If only he had taken a softer approach, that heart attack might have been averted. If only he had known about his father's preexisting condition. Well, whipping himself like this did not change the fact that he was right back where he had started: engaged to Rosa. His father's recovery had necessitated postponing the wedding, and he simply did not have the courage to confide in his stepmother. What a brutal blow it would have been to Carmenza! She had been happily immersing herself in special outfits and matching accessories ever since the official announcement was publicized. Fortunately, everyone else had been watching television in the farthest wing of the house when he and his father were on the stairs, and no one had heard the argument.

So, he had kept his mouth shut and, for now, he was stuck. For now? He felt that he was caught in a trap from which he would never escape. Once his father's condition improved, he would still insist that the wedding take place. What was he to do? Defy him again and risk a relapse? Of course, he didn't believe that threat to ruin his career. Such an action would boomerang on the family, and his father knew it. He had been bluffing. The heart attack, however, had been all too real. Again, he asked himself what he was to do. He walked on, racking his brain for some solution to a seemingly hopeless situation.

Finally, he dropped onto a bench, dejected. A cool breeze was stirring. His mind drifted to the woman in this very park. She might as well have been a figment of his imagination. He now knew that he would never see her again – and even if he did, what then?

Consciously, he had come here today to mentally resolve the conflict between himself and his father. Subconsciously, he had come to look for her. He could never come here without doing so. Guilt plagued him anew. He *would* forget her, and he would start by leaving this park right now and never returning.

He pushed himself to his feet, feeling terribly old! Short of going through with a marriage he dreaded, he could see no way out of the mess he was in.

He started walking briskly, forcibly emptying his mind of everything except appreciation of his immediate surroundings. Suddenly, he stopped, blinking in amazement. He could not believe it, but yes! There she was!

He sagged against a tree, his heart pounding. Was this what she had reduced him to – a weak-legged fool? And just what did he propose to do? Crawl to her on his hands and knees, begging for the privilege of one minute of her company? No, he would not! He would gather his courage about him like a man. He still had his pride – or did he? If he had any pride left, he would not risk rejection again. If he had any common sense, he would get away from here right now. At that moment, however, she looked up and saw him, and he couldn't move. He caught his breath. She was even more beautiful than he'd remembered, and she looked as shocked to see him as he was to see her!

CHAPTER 8

Sheila told herself that it couldn't be, but she knew it was the same man, and he looked as if he too had been taken off guard. He wasn't long in regaining his momentum. With brisk long strides, he moved toward her.

Conceited devil! Didn't he ever give up? Well, he would see, once and for all, that she wasn't interested in him. She stood up and swiftly headed for the other side of the park.

"Wait! Please!" he yelled.

Of all the nerve! He was following her! She began to run but, to her alarm, so did he. Setting her teeth, she propelled herself to a sudden burst of speed, widening the gap between them. She felt like whooping in triumph. This feeling was short-lived, however, because he wasn't giving up.

OK, mister. If it's a race you want, it's a race you'll get!

With the wind slapping her ears and the physical demands she was making on her body, it was as exhilarating as it once had been on the college track field.

"You don't – understand!" He sounded half-winded.

Oh, don't I? She grinned and glanced over her shoulder. He was gaining on her! Her legs began to ache from the strain, and her chest heaved rapidly as she gasped for air.

Her car was in sight. She pulled the keys from her pocket as she ran, determined to waste no time in getting away before he could reach her. But the moment she left the grass and touched the pavement, her left foot slid from under her. Instinctively, she flung out both arms in a vain attempt to keep her balance. One moment her arms were flailing; the next, she was flat on her back.

Her pursuer was beside her in seconds, bending over her with such a solicitous expression that the cutting words she'd so hastily rehearsed in her head died in her throat.

"Are you in pain?" he asked.

She nodded with a grimace.

"It's ... my right arm."

"Do not move."

He stood up, reached down to lift a mango peel from the sidewalk, and muttered "Imbeciles" as he strode away. Sheila couldn't have been more flabbergasted when he returned carrying a large, black leather case. He squatted beside her and flipped open the top of the case. Then, he extracted a small white pillow, which he placed under her head.

"Where did you get that?" Sheila asked in a pain-filled voice.

"From the trunk of my car. I always carry it in case of an emergency."

"You're a –," The word seemed to stick in her throat, and her eyes widened.

"A physician, yes. Now, let me see the arm," he said in a clipped, professional tone with a slight attractive accent. He probed; she winced. "Just below the elbow," he announced.

She cried out as he probed further.

"Easy," he murmured. "I will do my best to minimize your discomfort."

Sheila bit back the urge to retort that she'd like to minimize *him*.

He hailed a passing teenaged boy. The youth knelt beside the doctor and was instructed to take a plastic sleeve from the medical kit. He slid it onto Sheila's arm while Diego held the arm in a straight position. Then, continuing to follow instructions, the boy heartily blew into the rubber mouthpiece attached to the sleeve. The sleeve inflated, and the boy quickly twisted the mouthpiece shut to prevent air leakage. The doctor quickly cleaned the mouthpiece with a sanitary wipe and disposed of it in a small cellophane bag.

By this time, a nearby, curious crowd was increasing in size. Sheila was beginning to feel uneasy. The last thing she needed was to draw attention to herself.

"Any other sensitive areas?" the doctor asked.

"No," she replied.

"Then let's go." He helped her to her feet and motioned for the youth to carry the case.

"Where are you taking me?"

"To a clinic."

"My car —"

"Will be alright. For now, it is important to get your arm x-rayed."

As they crossed the road, Sheila stumbled. In the next instant, she was lifted into his arms.

"Put me down!" she protested.

"And risk your twisting an ankle?" he responded quietly.

"Nonsense."

"It was nonsense for you to run away from me back there."

Sheila pondered this for a moment as she scrutinized his face. The well-cut features set in an olive complexion and the thick raven-black hair had been noted with disdain and instantly dismissed the first time she'd seen him. In that foul mood, she had branded him a Latin wolf. Now, she studied the softly cleft chin, the sensuous mouth, the classically sculpted nose, the sooty long lashes, and the widely spaced brows. He *still* looked like a Latin wolf, even more so than before. Too handsome for his own good – and hers.

"Do I pass?" he asked.

"Frankly, no. You don't look like a doctor."

"No? What should a doctor look like?" He smiled down at her – a smile that lit up his dark eyes, revealed perfect teeth, and set her heart fluttering. "Well?" he prompted.

She squirmed, at a loss for words.

"*Bueno*, we have established one thing: I do not look like a doctor."

"You don't act like one either," she said, glaring up into his face.

"Don't I? Precisely how would you have treated the arm?"

"You can skip the sarcasm!" she snapped. "Doctors – decent doctors – don't harass women in parks."

"So, I am an indecent doctor who harasses women in parks. That is considerably more flattering than I dared hope for. You took off as if you thought me a rapist."

"All right, I overreacted. That doesn't excuse the fact that you were going to bother me again, knowing very well that I wanted to be left alone."

"Let me make one thing clear," he said, his voice edged in steel. "I spoke to you out of genuine concern. This park is not safe for a woman alone."

"I knew that," Sheila flatly stated.

"You knew?" he said in disbelief. "Then, why --?"

"I'll ask the questions. So, your only concern was for my safety?"

He didn't miss her cynical tone. He stiffened, determined not to reveal his attraction to her. "Yes, and pity," he levelly replied. "I could see that something was greatly troubling you. Your posture, and then your eyes. You had the saddest eyes I had ever seen."

"Do you also read palms?" she mocked. "For heaven's sake, where are you taking me?"

"As I already told you – to a clinic. My car is just over there."

"Mine is closer. You could use mine."

"And cut short the pleasure of having you in my arms?" His face was totally impassive, except for the twitch at the corners of his mouth, hinting at suppressed laughter.

She fumed in silence and, for the moment, he breathed a sigh of relief.

"Here we are," he announced, approaching a navy-blue Mustang. He carried her to the passenger side, gently set her on her feet, and unlocked the door. After carefully placing her in the passenger seat, he turned to the youth who had been following and extracted a generous number of peso notes from his wallet. The youth's profuse babblings of gratitude were almost pitiful to witness. He hurried off, his threadbare clothing testifying to his need for the money.

Diego deposited the medical case in the car's trunk and slid under the steering wheel.

Sheila was tense and nervous; it must have shown.

"Relax," the doctor said as he pulled away from the curb. "I'm a competent driver."

That appeared to be true, but even competency behind the wheel of a car didn't spare anyone from the daily challenges of driving among others with hot heads and short fuses. Before they arrived at the Clínica Palermo, they witnessed one driver hacking another's car roof with a machete in a lane in the opposite direction, where traffic had stalled. Even as a uniformed policeman approached, the offender continued his assault on the car while the apparently terrified victim remained inside his vehicle with the windows up and the doors locked. Just as the police officer approached, the offender raised his machete and charged forward. The Mustang quickly left the scene behind, but not before the crack of a pistol shot reached their ears.

!Qué *locura!"* Diego softly exclaimed.

What madness, indeed! Sheila silently agreed and was relieved when they pulled into the medical complex's parking lot.

CHAPTER 9

Sheila read the card for the third time:

Diego A. Santos-Aragón
Clínica Palermo
Avenida 42, No. 22-05, Bogotá, D.E.
Tel.: 285-2611 (consultorio), 256-0024 (residencia)

She fingered it again to convince herself that it was real. The man remained an enigma. He had excluded a title on the card, but he obviously was a medical doctor because he had driven her directly to the clinic, located not far from the park. There, several staff members respectfully addressed him as *Doctor Santos*. (In Colombia, the title "doctor" was often used for high society people, with or without medical degrees, but by the time she had undergone an X-Ray, and he had personally attended to her, she was convinced that he was genuine.) Then, exuding an air of utmost courtesy and professionalism, he drove her home.

She *had* misjudged him. The image of the sex-hungry man prowling parks for unescorted women faded before the reality of the self-confident physician. Yes, she had misjudged him badly, but she hadn't apologized. There was something about him, an aloofness that she dared not breach.

After unlocking the door of her apartment, he handed the keys to her.

"I'd completely forgotten about my car. I never even missed my keys."

"When you fell, so did the keys. I retrieved them and took the liberty of taking the car key off its ring and sending one of my staff to your car while you were having the arm X-rayed. Your doorman parked it in the garage."

"But I never gave you my address," Sheila remarked.

"I copied it and your telephone number from the standard form you filled out at the clinic," he stated.

"I must be rather scatter-brained."

"Understandable. You underwent a traumatic situation. I feel *almost* guilty that I chased you through the park."

"Almost?" she questioned.

"I do not regret chasing you, only that it ended in your being harmed," he said in the teasing tone he had used when he was carrying her out of the park.

"All's forgiven, Doctor," Sheila said, wondering where this was going. Probably nowhere since he would be leaving momentarily.

Once inside her chilly, damp apartment, he settled her on the sofa, started a blaze in the fireplace and found his way around her kitchen well enough to heat a can of minestrone soup and make a pot of coffee. His touch was feather-light as he arranged a soft wool blanket around her and placed the tray of soup and coffee on her lap. He then picked up the spoon from the tray, dipped it into the bowl, and brought it toward her mouth.

"What are you doing?" she gasped.

"At the clinic, I noticed that you had difficulty signing the documents with your left hand. Isn't it less of a struggle for you if I help?" he explained.

"Thank you, but I'm quite capable of feeding myself, even with my left hand," she stated, dumping the contents of the spoon back into the bowl as she took the spoon from him. "Besides, I'll have to get used to being self-sufficient – unless you plan to become my nurse until my arm heals."

"*Touché*, Miss Dunbar!" he rejoined with a smile – the same smile that had done strange things to her heart earlier and would again if she didn't get ahold of herself.

"*Ms.* Dunbar, if you please," Sheila corrected.

"You are ... married?" he asked.

"Dunbar is my maiden name. I'm divorced," she said, then added for good measure, "I have a son who is five."

"I see," he said, walking to the fireplace and holding out his hands to the blaze. He had turned his back to her, so she couldn't gauge the expression on his face. What was he thinking? His hands were shoved into his pockets, and his entire demeanor seemed to be one of deep contemplation as he stared down at the leaping flames.

In the next moment, the words were out of her mouth, uttered as if of their own volition, "You must be hungry too. You're welcome to heat up more soup."

His apparent pleasure lifted her mood. Shortly, he was sitting nearby with a tray on his lap. They ate in silence, and he finished long before she did.

"Uhm," he said, wiping his mouth with a paper napkin, "I had forgotten how good American soup could be, even from a can."

"You've been to the States?"

"I received my medical training from Columbia University. New York City can be bitterly cold. I practically breathed hot canned soup every winter, all winter long."

He stood up, consulted his watch, then looked at her with concern.

"Do you live here alone?"

"Yes," she replied, feeling strangely bereft by this forewarning of his imminent departure.

"You said that you have a son."

"That's true, but he's in the States. My mother is caring for him until this assignment is over.

"I have heard of how stringent security measures are now at the US Embassy."

"And for the staff at all our mission locations."

"It will be difficult for you to manage any routine tasks with your right arm out of commission. Have you no help here?"

"A maid. She comes in twice a week to clean, but I do my own cooking – oh!"

He rushed to her side and knelt to peer into her face. "Is your arm hurting?"

"No. I just remembered. I've invited thirty people for a buffet tomorrow. The maid won't be able to make it because of a death in her family. It's too late to hire someone else on such short notice, so I decided to handle everything by myself. Now this!" Her voice trailed off in dismay.

"Listen," he said, "I know someone who may be available. I hear that she is an excellent cook. On the other hand, it might be wise to postpone the event until you are better."

"It's rather late for that. It would inconvenience those I've invited. So, if you think someone could help me on such short notice, I'd appreciate your calling them. There's a phone in the kitchen."

He took the trays, entered the kitchen, made a call, and quickly rinsed the few dishes in hot water before returning to the living room to inform her that Lucy was on her way.

"Well," she commented, "I've taken up enough of your precious time. I'm sure you have more important things to do."

"Not at all. It is just that I am on call this evening, and I hope to get a nap before it gets very busy, as it tends to do on most late Saturday nights."

Promising to check on her later, he handed her his card and hurried away.

Lucy Dickens arrived around four o'clock that afternoon. To Sheila's surprise, she was from the Colombian island of San Andrés where English is commonly spoken. A tall, cinnamon-complexioned young woman with a thick black braid pinned to one side of her head, she explained that she was a student at National University and was glad to earn extra cash whenever she could. She quoted an hourly rate that was quite reasonable, then got busy in the kitchen, following Sheila's instructions carefully. She worked steadily for three hours, singing softly, then announced, "Preliminaries are done. What time should I arrive tomorrow?"

"One-thirty will be fine. Guests are invited for three."

After Lucy left, Sheila contemplated the card on the coffee table. Then, telling herself to *give it a rest*, she got up, brushed her teeth, and struggled into her nightgown.

She lay in bed, all lights out, wide awake. Would Dr. Santos call as he had promised? A fractured arm didn't require a lot of care, did it? Any phone call from him would be one of mere courtesy.

Her eyelids began to droop. She wondered exactly what the relationship between Lucy and the doctor might be. Were they more than friends? *And if they are, what's it to you?* she chided herself.

She deliberately turned her thoughts to Kevin — mischievous, lovable Kevin. What she wouldn't give for one of his hugs right now, even if she could only hug him back with one arm, for the other was beginning to throb! She peered through the darkness at her radio clock. It was ten and time for another painkiller. She switched on the bedside lamp and reached for the pill bottle.

The telephone rang, setting her heart thumping. She cleared her throat and answered it on the third ring.

"Ms. Dunbar? Dr. Santos. How are you feeling?"

"Not very well. I was just going to take a couple of pills."

"Fine, but remember what I said."

"No more than two tablets every six hours, then after the first day, two every eight hours," she quoted.

"Right. Tell me, what do you think of Lucy?"

"She's a God-send. How can I ever thank you?"

"An invitation to your event would be sufficient," he casually suggested.

"My ... event?" she said, stunned.

"On the other hand, I would not wish to intrude –"

"No, no, not at all, Doctor. It's just that I assumed your schedule might not allow it."

"Unless my colleague on duty becomes ill himself, I will be free."

"Then, I'll expect you around three."

"Three? Until tomorrow then. Rest well, Ms. Dunbar."

"Thank you, Doctor. Good night."

Sheila replaced the receiver with a trembling hand. No, she wasn't going to stay awake trying to figure out the man's motive for inviting himself to her buffet or start analyzing the reason for her apprehension at the very thought of his presence there. No man was worth losing sleep over.

CHAPTER 10

"Calm down. I won't eat you, although I may be tempted to nibble. You're a knockout, even with one arm out of whack."

Brad Davis, an Assistant Regional Security Officer, towered over her, bending his head to whisper in her ear. He was a good-looking tall bachelor who, since his arrival at post six weeks ago, had his eyes on Sheila. This invitation today was just the boost his flagging ego needed. He told himself that it wasn't as if she could afford to be choosy. He was one of only four Black American men serving at the embassy. The other three were a twenty-year-old Marine Corps guard named Danny Robinson; Elton Wilkes, a young gay office manager assigned to the Economic Section; and John Thompson, the Administrative Officer, a widower in his mid-forties who looked older than his age because of prematurely graying hair. So, Davis concluded that he was *the* eligible one, and Sheila knew it but was playing hard-to-get. Well, he would bide his time. She couldn't hold out much longer. He stepped back and eyed her from head to toe. Wow!

"You're embarrassing me," Sheila informed him in a low voice.

"Sorry, but, baby, I can't help myself," Brad remarked in the tone of one at the end of his patience.

"Please try," Sheila said, moving away to circulate among her other guests. She was well aware that his eyes followed her. From the moment they'd been introduced, she'd known that he was attracted to her. He was cute, but Sheila conceded that his lines sounded a bit too rehearsed to be sincere. She enjoyed male admiration as much as any woman, but it would be all too easy to be bowled over by someone like Brad. She had no intention of rushing into anything. It might be interesting to first find out what lay beneath that attractive exterior and the smooth talk.

Annoyance vied with nerves as four o'clock approached, and there was still no sign of the Colombian doctor. At five after four, the doorman buzzed the intercom. Sheila was glad that her boss's wife, Liz, offered to answer it. If it were the doctor, she at least would have time to compose herself, although she couldn't understand why she was nervous.

"Hey, Sheila! Do you know a Diego Santos?" Liz called out.

"Yes. Tell the doorman to send him up."

She listened to the muted whir of the elevator, and her pulses bounded. When it stopped at her floor and he stepped off, she was at the door to greet him with what she hoped was a coolness she was far from feeling.

"Hi. Glad you could make it," she said.

"I am sorry to be late. I had to make an unexpected call at the clinic on my way here. How is the arm today?"

"Better. Come on in. Let me introduce you to everybody."

He looked distinguished in a pinstriped navy suit, paisley tie, and white shirt, which contrasted well with his olive complexion. He also looked out of place as Sheila had forgotten to inform him that it was to be a casual event. However, if he was uncomfortable, he didn't show it. He acknowledged each introduction with the low-key manner of someone accustomed to frequent socializing. Sheila noticed the heightened interest his arrival was causing among the ladies, whose reactions ranged from discreet glances to open flirtations.

Brad's reception of the newcomer was polite but chilly. Until this Diego Santos came, he had been the focus of several women. Now, Santos was getting all the attention, and he didn't like it. Who would have thought to see the outdated European custom of kissing the hostess's hand in this day and age? What a phony the guy was!

The buffet was a success. Lucy was indispensable. Almost everyone had second portions. A few of the guests complained about the lack of "hard stuff," but most of them seemed satisfied with what was offered. One of the Colombian couples opened the dancing, moving in perfect unison to the lively rhythms of the *salsa*, then the *cumbia*. The doctor danced with Liz. Brad abruptly pulled Sheila to his chest. Startled, she drew back.

"Come on, loosen up," he said with a grin.

"I could say the same to you. I won't vanish into thin air," she upbraided him.

"Yeah, I know. You're *all* woman!" he growled huskily into her ear.

Since Sheila had neither a ready answer nor the desire to encourage him, she said nothing.

As the music ended, he asked, "What are you doing tomorrow night?"

"May I?" Diego Santos broke in, just behind Brad.

Brad shrugged and stepped aside, muttering, "Sure."

Sheila was hesitant to dance with the doctor. As the hostess, she shouldn't favor one guest over another. However, Brad hadn't seemed to mind monopolizing her time and giving the impression that the two of them were already intimately involved. In a way, she was relieved that the doctor had intervened.

As the Spanish rendition of the Julio Iglesias hit "Hey" floated over the air and she moved into the doctor's arms, she completely forgot about Brad. The touch of Diego's gentle hands on her back and the soft fanning of his breath in her hair had a tantalizing effect on Sheila. She admitted to herself that she was enjoying the moment. He was only a couple of inches taller than she was, and Sheila couldn't resist looking into his face. In the same instant, he was looking down, and their eyes met. Sheila quickly looked away, her heart jerking in response to his warm gaze. What had gotten into her? She kept her eyes averted for the rest of their dance together and primly thanked him when it was over.

Brad claimed her for the next number, a slow *vallenato*, but there was none of the excitement she had felt with the doctor.

"What are you afraid of?" he teased.

"Nothing," came her firm reply.

"Yet you're as stiff as a board."

"I guess I'm just tired," Sheila stated, hoping she sounded convincing.

"Ha-ha!" Brad laughed. "I'll believe that when my grandma wears a bikini!"

"Brad, don't you think you're moving a little too fast? We hardly know each other."

"We'll have to work on that, won't we? But how well do you know Diego Santos?"

"We met just recently," Sheila replied.

"I'll bet he'd like to be a lot more than your doctor," he said with a lopsided smile.

"Oh please!" she cried, a note of disgust in her voice.

Obviously satisfied with her reaction, Brad continued, "He's not your type, baby. Now, about tomorrow night —"

"Pardon me," a voice behind him quietly intoned. It was Santos again. "Ms. Dunbar, may I speak with you for a moment?"

Brad's face mirrored his irritation. "Can't it wait?"

"Regrettably, it cannot. Please excuse us," the doctor stated, placing a hand on Sheila's elbow. As they moved out of Brad's hearing, he asked, "Is there a place where we can talk privately?"

Sheila nodded and led the way to a small study. Once inside, the doctor turned to lock the door.

"What's this about?" she asked with widened eyes.

Diego wasted no time in getting to the point. "I believe one of your guests may have a serious health issue."

"Who is it?" Sheila asked.

"He identified himself as the Commercial Counselor."

"That's Paul Landers. It's well-known that he has a pretty low opinion of conventional medicine. We're required to have physical checkups at intervals between assignments – at least Foreign Service employees are. We're under the direction of the US Department of State, but not all embassy staff are. Mr. Landers is a Department of Commerce officer. There may be some slack in their regulations. Do you think the issue could be serious?"

"Yes, I am fairly certain of it. There is a sizable mole on his left inner wrist that shows all the signs of melanoma. I think he should have it examined as soon as possible."

"And you told him so?" Sheila asked.

"As tactfully as I could. He was not receptive to the idea."

There was a brief silence as they both mulled over what else could be done.

"I suppose I could talk to his wife," Sheila said. "She might have more sway over him than either you or I would."

"Will you – right away?" Diego asked with an air of urgency.

"Of course. I think I last saw her heading for more dessert. She has quite a sweet tooth."

"Thank you, Ms. Dunbar. Let us hope that I do not have to do a second diagnosis – for indigestion," he said with a grin as he unlocked the door of the study.

"In that case, I'm afraid you'd have more patients to diagnose than Mrs. Landers," Sheila said as they stepped back into the living room. Half the guests had converged on the buffet table. A few had their plates piled so high that Sheila was glad she had set out the dinner-sized porcelain plates instead of the smaller buffet ones.

They chuckled heartily before going their separate ways, Sheila to speak to Mrs. Landers and Diego to circulate among other guests.

The shared laughter between them did not go unnoticed by Brad Davis. He caught Sheila's left arm as she headed toward Mrs. Landers.

"Hey, what's the rush? What about tomorrow night?" he asked.

"Tomorrow? Oh, tomorrow! I guess I forgot. Right now, I need to talk to Mrs. Landers. It's rather important. Will you excuse me?"

His grip on her arm tightened, but he tried to inject a note of lightness into his voice. "Only if you promise to come back for another dance."

"I promise," Sheila said, her tone solemn but her mind fully occupied with Diego's concern about the Commercial Counselor.

Brad released her, stepped back and, feeling rather deserted, watched as she made her way across the room to Mrs. Landers.

From Brad's vantage point, Sheila's conversation with Portia Landers appeared to be quite intense. It lasted a lot longer than he thought it would. Sheila seemed to be trying to persuade the older woman about something, even pleading with her. Finally, the woman must have agreed. Sheila was rewarded with a nod and a hug.

Sheila was turning away now, searching – probably for him. He raised his arm and started toward her, eager for the promised dance; but to his extreme irritation, Diego Santos stepped into her line of vision and steered her out onto the apartment balcony.

Well, if he thought Brad was going to play second fiddle, he could think again! By the time he slid back the balcony door, their foreheads were almost touching as if they were sharing a secret. It was all he could do to keep from jerking the other man away from his woman – for that's how he'd already come to regard Sheila. Instead, he cleared his throat and asked with a contrived smile, "May I join the party?"

There was only a slight pause before Sheila graciously replied, "Sure. I believe I promised you a dance."

"That you did," he reminded her with a look of satisfaction which quickly disappeared when she turned toward the doctor and asked, "Wait for me?"

"I will be here," he firmly assured her.

Unfortunately, the hit "Querida" by popular Mexican singer Juan Gabriel was playing when she voiced her refusal to go out with Brad. The slow rhythm and mournful lyrics seemed to spur him into almost savage behavior as he clasped her so tightly to him that she could hardly breathe.

"Brad, please!"

"Brad, please!" he mimicked in a high falsetto, then laughed as if he knew she was simply toying with him. "Oh, come on, Sheila, you're not being fair. Give me a chance – just one chance to take you out. Is that too much for a brother to ask?"

So, he's going to use that "I'm Black, you're Black, you owe me" tactic, Sheila was thinking, but reluctantly consented. "All right."

Having gotten the answer he wanted, Brad ended the dance with a quick sweep of his fingers across the nape of her neck, which sent a shiver of repulsion up her spine and made her regret agreeing to go out with him. Perhaps he was the kind of guy who wasn't used to being rejected by women, but he was trying *too* hard. He *was* cute, but she was beyond the days of getting giddy over looks alone. Well, she might as well get it over with, or he'd probably not let up. He was picking her up tomorrow night at eight o'clock. For now, she was anxious to return to the balcony. It turned out that she and Diego Santos shared a common interest in the Bible as well as a love of Caribbean cuisine.

As she stepped out onto the balcony again, she was disappointed to see that the doctor had been joined by Christy Welles, a Junior Officer from the Consular Section. It was apparent that the issuance of passports and visas was the last thing on her mind. The young, green-eyed blonde might have just left the stage of a beauty contest. Where men were concerned, she certainly knew how to play up her physical assets. In essence, she seemed enthralled by the doctor. Was she as determined to capture him as Brad was to snare Sheila?

****

Diego had disliked Christy on sight. Granted, she looked like a movie star in a low-cut peasant blouse, long legs encased in skin-tight jeans, and heavily applied makeup. But she was also too forward, too artificial, and too vain. Her eyes belied any sweetness beneath those honeyed tones. They were dissecting eyes. He could feel them dissecting him now.

"So, you're a doctor," she said.

"Yes, I am."

"Specialist?"

"Oncologist. I'm very much interested in research. However, I mostly practice general medicine."

"What's holding you back?" Christy asked.

"One is compelled to serve where the need is greatest," he explained.

"Ooh, an idealist!" she crooned, raising a well-arched brow. Then, as if just noticing Sheila, she said, "Oh, hi, Sheila! The doctor and I were just getting better acquainted."

"Fascinating, isn't he?" Sheila boldly commented.

"Tell me, Diego – you don't mind if I call you Diego," Christy said, then without waiting for a response, continued, "How did you and Sheila meet?"

Sheila's breathing suspended while she hoped that Diego would not mention *where* they met.

"I was the attending physician," he vaguely replied.

"So, your relationship is new?"

To Sheila's astonishment, Diego stepped to her side and gazed forlornly down into her eyes. "Sadly, yes, but I look forward to knowing her much better."

Suddenly, the fiery notes of Jamaican reggae punctured the air, and he became all gallantry and charm. "May I have this dance, Sheila?"

"I'd love to!" she gushed, mentally noting: *We should have been actors.*

"With your permission," Diego said with a slight bow to Christy before taking Sheila's hand at precisely the moment Brad Davis slid open the balcony door. Christy and Brad stood there dumbfounded by this turn of events. But to everyone's amazement, despite the music's reggae rhythm, the lyrics spoke of God's greatness. More amazing were the number of couples taking to the floor. This was thanks to Lucy who, apart from serving, followed Sheila's instruction to slip that attention-grabbing disc onto the player, although Sheila wondered how many were really listening to the lyrics.

As evening fell, Sheila could not help but wish her guests would begin dispersing, but they seemed to be in no hurry to leave. She, on the other hand, was exhausted, and a dull throb was radiating up her injured arm. After the Jamaican praise song, Diego consulted his wristwatch and announced, "You are due another dosage of the pain medication in a few minutes. She nodded but had no chance to say anything because what happened next took everyone by surprise. Lights flickered. A deep rumble and tremendous shaking ensued, causing dishes to clatter, furniture to slide, and the entire apartment building to sway.

Someone screamed, "It's an earthquake!" and four of the new American staff ran toward the door, intent on escaping as fast as they could. However, Patrick Carmichael and Witt Jones, the Regional Security Officer, were intentionally blocking their way. Pat asked where they thought they were going.

"To the elevator!" Babs Benson, a newcomer to the Foreign Service, gasped.

"The worst place you could go," Pat informed her.

"You can't keep us here!" shouted Junior Officer Vince Proctor, raising his fist, but Brad was already upon him, pinning both arms behind his back.

"You mustn't panic. Remember what you learned in orientation. Stairs, not elevators. But you'll be safer waiting it out right here," he said in a deep, authoritative tone which seemed to calm those who had rushed toward the door.

Then, as suddenly as they had started, the tremors stopped.

CHAPTER 11

Country Team meetings, an administrative staple of US embassies around the world, were usually held weekly. At the US Embassy in Bogotá, they occasionally convened more often because of the heightened security situation in the country. The Monday after Sheila's party was one such occurrence, having, up to this point, been chaired by Mr. Brighton, the temporary head of the embassy, who had just departed for home leave and his next tour of duty in Sweden.

This morning's meeting was attended by most of the embassy's section heads and chaired by Rick Váldez, the new US Ambassador to the Republic of Colombia. He had arrived only three weeks ago and, of course, had already been briefed on all the latest happenings at post. He was a diminutive man with steel-gray hair, a caramel complexion, and Aztec features. His piercing brown eyes had been known to strike terror into many a subordinate, for he more than made up in assertiveness what he lacked in stature. Nevertheless, the Ambassador could not abide snobbery. He was not a political appointee who'd bought his position from the US President. However, one never knew what to expect. Some political appointees were surprisingly efficient and effective – not afraid to consult with experienced officers in order to accomplish the mission, while others and a few regular diplomats turned out to be *empty suits*.

On this occasion, his first meeting with the staff, he appeared quite cordial, his eyes belying nothing of the iron will within. Behind the seemingly casual survey of his diplomatic staff was a sweeping mental assessment of each one.

He never judged anyone on the basis of mere physical appearance or, for that matter, the time-worn and what he considered inadequate tests of a handshake and a direct look into the eyes. No, he left nothing to conjecture. He'd reviewed all the personnel files he could get his hands on. He had also gleaned much from Brighton, then personally visited each section chief.

Now he matched the faces to the noted profiles of each:

Patrick Carmichael, Counselor for Political Affairs. An extremely capable and hardworking officer with ten years in the Foreign Service. His political reporting in Kabul, Baghdad, and New Delhi had earned him superior evaluations and meritorious awards. Having had a few close brushes with death, he consistently hit the ground running at every post. Váldez appreciated such competency and tenacity in his officers. Carmichael was on track for the next rung of the career ladder -- Deputy Chief of Mission and, eventually, an ambassadorship. Váldez did not doubt it.

Next to Carmichael sat Peter Sweetwater, Counselor for Economic Affairs. Why the staff nicknamed him Sweet Pete was a mystery to the Ambassador. Sweetwater had been competent as a younger officer, but a weakness for drink had robbed him of a once-brilliant mind. At best, he was now mediocre. Still, he had to hand it to Sweetwater. He had availed himself of the

Department's alcoholism counseling program and had made commendable progress despite relapsing from time to time. Unfortunately, those relapses always coincided with relapses in the quality of his work. At fifty-six, with more than twenty-two years in the service, Sweetwater certainly met the criteria for retirement, and Váldez would see that he was nudged in that direction.

John Thompson, Counselor for Administrative Affairs, was amiable, hardworking, and very capable. A Black man with twelve years of service in the corps, he was perhaps the most straightforward of the entire staff. A widower whose wife had encouraged him to follow his dreams, he had known great success as an opera singer, performing in all the great houses of Europe – until she perished in a helicopter crash and, reportedly, Thompson lost interest in the opera world. He was an outstanding administrator. Selfishly, the Ambassador hoped he would not regain his interest in singing opera– at least not until his tour here ended. In the meantime, Váldez intended to take full advantage of Thompson's talents at official dinners and other diplomatic events. He might be persuaded to render a few easy-listening songs.

Rod Radcliff, Consul General. Sixtyish, on the verge of retiring, and someone who would not be missed. He was a typical *empty suit* who had become far too complacent over the years. Then there was his tendency to crack down on the Foreign Service nationals (locally hired Colombians) while often letting the American staff slack off. In fact, a reliable source had informed the Ambassador that a bombshell named Christy practically had Radcliff wrapped around her little finger. That was one reason the Consular Section was behind in handling its passport and visa requests. Váldez's newly arrived Deputy Chief of

Mission, Sandra Charlemagne, would ensure that the section soon got up to speed, no two ways about it. Charlemagne had a reputation for getting results. That's why he had requested that she, instead of a less experienced DCM, be assigned here.

Thatcher Temple, General Services Officer, did his job well, which was about all that could be said of him – except the nickname of "Temper" which he got from exploding if any lower-ranking employee dared interfere with his sports obsession on the weekends. Yet, he had shown time and time again that an order conveyed by his superiors was not to be second-guessed, but complied with promptly. But for an injury in the NFL, he would still be a football linebacker.

Paul Landers, Commercial Counselor, was looking as disgruntled as he probably felt. He was a capable officer, but had the reputation of sometimes going against the grain. It was rumored that he had missed a few of his recommended physical exams because of mistrust of conventional medicine. Well, each person, specifically those of other agencies, must let their conscience be their guide in such matters. He, Váldez, had no intention of pressuring Landers unless the efficient operation of the US Mission here was being negatively impacted.

Grover Paxton, the Budget and Fiscal Officer, was excellent in his field but was not a reliable pinch hitter. He was a sharp, first-rate accountant, but placed in some other section, he would be (and had been) like a fish out of water. He had a reputation of seldom smiling these days, especially since his wife and toddler had departed post. It seemed he coped with the loneliness by working harder than ever, almost to the point of perpetual exhaustion. Now *that* was a staff situation the

Ambassador rarely had to contend with during his decades of service.

Sally Brandt, Chief of the US Information Service, was the only woman in this group. She wore tailored slacks and jackets, flat lace-up shoes, oversized wire-rimmed glasses, no makeup, and a limp, shaggy hairdo. She was of medium height, nicely proportioned, and could be physically appealing if she chose to be, which she apparently did not. Rumors were circulating with regard to her sexuality, which Váldez personally couldn't care less about. Of primary importance was the fact that she did her job well, kept her head down, and minded her own business. He had every intention of reminding his staff to do the same.

Regional Security Officer Witt Jones was a former FBI Special Agent whose opinion of himself was a bit too lofty to suit the Ambassador. Yet his performance was consistently beyond reproach and up to any challenge. Except for the Superman syndrome, he would be a more likable officer. Perhaps a little less excitement was just what he needed. In the meantime, the newest addition to the Regional Security Office, under Jones's supervision, might be of some cause for concern (and thus discipline). Ambassador Váldez, from a review of Brad Davis's file, noted with interest that he had been reprimanded at two previous posts – not for dereliction of duty. In fact, his annual evaluations were always "excellent." Of concern was Davis's tendency to project a less-than-professional image among the host-country citizens during his off-duty hours. Details were scarce in his file, but his description as a "playboy" did not bode well for his upward mobility in the service. He would bear close watching.

All along the table, Váldez proceeded, weighing and sizing up each officer, but so quickly that no one suspected what he was doing. Most of these officers were talented and hardworking, with a few noted exceptions. There were a few non-State Department notables in this staff meeting whose brief presentations he would encourage but not spend an inordinate amount of time on. That excluded Ty Collier, head of the Drug Enforcement Administration (DEA) detail. His agency had lost a Special Agent recently, one who had been targeted and gunned down in Barranquilla by a well-known cartel operative. Váldez was well aware of how such a loss could bring down morale, not only among DEA employees but the entire mission staff. The Ambassador must be the one to set a positive tone while reminding everyone that vigilance and adherence to security regulations were the main keys to safety. He was confident that his own tour of duty in Colombia would be one of the most memorable since entering the Foreign Service Corps twenty-five years ago as a Junior Officer at the US Embassy in Yaoundé, Cameroon.

The Ambassador glanced at his watch and cleared his throat. The assembled group took the hint and fell silent. Despite his toughness, he could be affable when he chose to be. Today, he chose to be affable, for starters.

He began by commending Carmichael and Jones for their quick actions at a recent event, which had reduced panic during the earthquake and, thus, prevented harm to some of the staff. Then, he listened to reports from the various sections, calling on the Regional Security Officer last.

Witt Jones gave a summary of the latest events. Then, drawing himself up to his full six feet six inches, he informed his colleagues, "That about wraps it up. Everything's pretty much under control from our end. We'll keep you apprised of any new developments."

As he started to take his seat, the Ambassador made a detaining gesture. "Just a moment, Mr. Jones. You mentioned the abduction of a young American geologist, James Robert Stephenson, two weeks ago. What's being done to secure his release?"

Jones looked somewhat taken aback for a moment, then rubbed his hands together before responding, "Well, Mr. Ambassador, his company, PENCO, has sent a couple of their own security people down here from its Dallas headquarters to try negotiating with the kidnappers."

"And –?"

"So far, they've come to no agreement on the amount of ransom demanded."

"And they – the negotiating team – have they been in direct contact with you?"

"Of course, sir," Jones replied. "The victim's family, understandably, wants answers."

"May I then deduce that you have informed them of the US Government's policy with regard to American citizens taken hostage?" Váldez asked.

"Well, yes, Mr. Ambassador, but –"

"The President has made it quite clear – and our legislators agree – that our government will pay no ransom for the release of American citizens taken hostage. Do I have your assurance that you will firmly reiterate this to the negotiators?"

"Yes, sir, but – you see, these big corporations pay millions every year in insurance to cover themselves for situations such as this. If they're willing to pay ransom to get their employees back, then there's nothing we can do to stop them. There's no federal law prohibiting private entities from paying ransom."

"Mr. Jones, I'm well aware of both the kidnap insurance and our laws. However, the paying of ransom only increases the potential for future kidnappings. These terrorists start getting bolder, and they begin looking for the next victim. A precedent is set, and the cycle never ends. The ransom is used to buy arms in furtherance of other illicit operations. Regardless of PENCO's intentions, it is imperative that the company understand the official US position. I want no ambiguity bandied about in the press that might even link our position to whatever action PENCO might take. Get in touch with the negotiators today."

"That may be difficult, sir."

"Do your best, Mr. Jones. Try to set up a meeting with them this week. In fact, I personally would like to meet with their head negotiator – if you can arrange it."

"I'll do my best, Mr. Ambassador," he said, starting toward his seat.

Again, Ambassador Váldez motioned for him to remain standing. "There is one final matter of concern this morning," he announced. "Whose *bright* idea was it to have that party yesterday?" he demanded in a biting tone that startled them all.

Patrick Carmichael spoke up, "My office manager, Sheila Dunbar, hosted it, Mr. Ambassador."

"I believe that Ms. Dunbar is a support person, *not* a section head," Váldez stated. "*Who* is responsible for the safety of the staff at this mission – for both direct-hire staff and host-country nationals?"

Everyone present knew the question was rhetorical. All heads turned in the direction of Witt Jones, who blushed to the roots of his ginger-hued hair.

"I am, Mr. Ambassador," he said.

"Mr. Jones, I arrived here only three weeks ago, but I'm no rookie and, as a seasoned officer with two previous assignments in security under your belt, neither should you be. Beirut is the most dangerous post on the planet. Bogotá, as you know, is number two – for a reason. And yet, I was informed that over thirty of our people – and an unknown local – were at that party. More than thirty people gathered in *one* place, potentially prime targets for a massacre. Those thirty did *not* include the two bodyguards that the RSO had on duty *downstairs*, I assume, as a *necessary* precaution." This last was delivered dryly as his eyes bored into those of the RSO with laser-like precision before he continued, "This scenario, ladies – pardon, lady – and gentlemen, smacks of laxness. Laxness is the one thing we cannot afford at this post. It is the one attitude I will *not* tolerate!"

The Ambassador's eyes circled the table and seemed to pierce the thoughts of each person there. However, it was to Witt Jones that he directed his final remarks.

"We all volunteered to serve at this post. We are *not* here to become noble heroes. *Neither* are we here to become the latest collateral-damage statistics in this war on drugs and terrorism. There are to be *no* more parties at this post until further notice, which may be a very long time in coming. My staff will plan official state-level dinners and other events efficiently, but these activities must also be monitored with utmost care. Mr. Jones, update our security policy and see to it that all staff members are briefed thoroughly. That especially includes the direct-hire staff. No laxness in the rules that already exist. They are to keep their radios with them at all times, maintain strict secrecy of their code names, prearrange taxi rides and fares, avoid riding buses altogether, be careful whom they associate with during nonduty hours, et cetera. I want a copy of the revised policy on my desk by tomorrow at noon. Understood, Mr. Jones?"

"Understood, Mr. Ambassador," Jones staunchly replied.

Suddenly, the granite-like features of Ambassador Váldez melted into those of a benevolent uncle. He smiled, wished them all a "great week," and exited the conference room with a jaunty air that left the entire group amazed.

A few minutes later, Patrick Carmichael was giving Sheila the highlights of the Country Team meeting.

"Security, security, security," he said as if weary of the topic. "As if we haven't heard it all before. A revised policy is coming out tomorrow. No more parties, I'm afraid."

Sheila was secretly relieved and chose not to comment on this latest information.

He took the political report he was holding to his safe and carefully placed it inside. One would have thought it a portfolio instead of the actual two-page summary that it was.

"Everybody gets up, presents their reports, and then Jones steals the show as usual – at least until the Ambassador gives him a dressing down about allowing your party."

Sheila tried to conceal her amusement over the professional jealousy behind his mood. Her boss didn't like Witt Jones, although they seemed cordial and cooperative when they had to work together. Witt had an inflated opinion of his own importance, but he wasn't fabricating the dangers to keep himself in the limelight. Security was *the* issue of interest among the staff these days, and it was natural that the new Ambassador would prioritize it.

"Oh, well, Pat, when the security situation stabilizes someday, you'll get your chance to shine again," she consoled.

Carmichael caught a glimpse of a dimple and snorted, "Sheila, I believe you're poking fun at me."

"Now, why would I do a thing like that?" she asked, looking patently innocent.

"Because, first, you know the security situation isn't likely to stabilize anytime soon and, secondly, you love to rib me."

"Why, Pat! I? Rib you? I'd just as soon rib the Ambassador himself!" she exclaimed.

"And you would, you fox!" he said with a chuckle, his bad mood dissolving.

"OK," Sheila said with a grin, "I confess, but I only did it to cheer you up. You've been like a sore-headed bear lately."

"You're right. It must be this high altitude and gloomy weather we've been having lately."

"And the security situation?" she teased.

"Now, don't start that again. We got an earful of it this morning. Personally, I don't think things are as bad as Jones would have us all believe — the worst is probably behind us — but then, he's got to keep himself in the spotlight."

Sheila yawned dramatically and asked, "Do I detect a hint of –?"

"All right," Carmichael said, throwing up both hands and laughing. "You got me again."

Just then, the telephone rang.

Sheila's usual cordial "Political Section, good morning!" faded to a more serious tone as the caller wasted no time on niceties.

She hung up and crisply announced, "Pat, the Ambassador would like to see you – immediately."

"Just when I was getting into a good mood," her boss remarked.

"Positive thoughts, boss," Sheila encouraged.

"Of course. You know me: Mr. Sunshine," he said as he headed out the door.

It was Sheila who laughed then.

Meanwhile, just outside Calí, Colombia at a special training camp in the mountains, two young M-19 commandos drilled the Ivan Marino squadron on a plan that would take them to the capital city on a "great mission." The youthful faces of over two dozen men and eight women burned with maniacal fervor. Visions of glory swept aside any fear of danger. One thought reigned supreme in their minds: they would win! Whatever the cost, they would win!

CHAPTER 12

Brad Davis turned women's heads wherever he went. He liked to think that Elvis's "A hunk, a hunk of burning love" described him perfectly. He was handsome, and knew it, as did all the women he encountered. They usually came to him willingly – eagerly – and he liberally partook of what was offered and moved on with seldom a thought of committing himself to a long-term relationship. He had had women of every color, race, and ethnicity. Single, married, separated, widowed, divorced – it made no difference to him. It was inevitable, therefore, that so many easy sexual conquests would make him conceited.

By day, he perpetuated the image of a congenial and capable young diplomat. By night, he unleashed the playboy side of himself. He loved women. He couldn't get enough of them, and they couldn't get enough of him – or so it seemed until he met Sheila Dunbar. From that moment on, he'd wanted her as he'd never wanted any woman before. Both being Black would work in his favor, so that he could quickly get her exactly where he wanted her: in bed. However, things hadn't gone according to plan. Night after night, he consoled himself with other women – and remained oddly unsatisfied. He forced himself to wait, but patience had never been one of his virtues. Friendly chats with her in the halls and the embassy cafeteria brought him no closer to his goal. Then, at last, an invitation to her buffet gave him reason to hope.

Initially, he thought that the arrival of the Colombian doctor would pose a threat to him, but she had agreed to a date with him that very next night. He immediately realized, however, that she would be neither a quick nor easy conquest. So, he would bide his time, and when he snared her, she would be well worth the wait!

Brad took Sheila out to a movie, then dropped her off at her apartment, pretending to have an early and long next-day schedule before heading not to his apartment but to a club that catered to strippers and *ladies of the night*. This strategy seemed to work because she agreed to a second date with him. He treated her to dinner at one of the city's more exclusive restaurants famous for its French cuisine. Once again, he was a perfect gentleman, citing the demands of a heavy workload the next day. Little fool that she was, she fell for it and was sweetly understanding – just like putty in his hands. Surely, the third date would be the charm to deliver the *prize* he so desperately wanted. Congratulating himself on his upcoming coup, he decided to let her salivate for a week before asking her out again. Yet how elusive that third date was proving to be! She declined his invitations twice. Was she interested in Santos after all? He refused to believe that she could prefer the Colombian to him. Time and time again, he'd seen for himself that Black women were extremely loyal to their own race, definitely a point in his favor. There certainly was nothing black about Santos except the color of his hair. So, why had Sheila been putting him off lately?

****

Meanwhile, Sheila pondered her refusal of that third date with Brad. She supposed she should be flattered by his attentions. He was good-looking, well educated, and fun loving; but was that enough? She remained doubtful.

She wanted to like Brad. Because of a shared racial history, she'd assumed that they would have some cultural interests and values in common. This was disappointingly untrue. From the way he had ogled her, his only attraction to her was physical – or was she misjudging him? Her suspicions might be unfair; after all, wasn't he young and entitled to be carefree and unburdened with serious matters when he was off duty? Maybe that was his way of coping with this stressful assignment.

Still, she remained leery. Perhaps she should have followed her first intuition and not agreed to go out with him. God forbid he should think that she was simply stringing him along!

Sheila was relieved when he called to say that he was going on temporary duty to Lima, Peru. He would be there for at least a month, filling in until a newly assigned Assistant Security Officer arrived at post.

Little did she suspect that in his absence, her relationship with Diego Santos would take an unexpected turn during the remaining months of her assignment.

CHAPTER 13

Christy Welles loved living overseas. She particularly enjoyed being assigned to Bogotá. Once the "no minors at post" policy was implemented because of the dangers to American diplomats, as well as their children, the number of men without wives and children at post swelled, meaning, of course, a larger dating pool. Christy had no qualms about dating married men, but she was most interested in the one who could advance her career: her immediate supervisor, Consular Section Chief Rod Radcliff. In another year, he likely would be retiring just as she'd be transferring to another post. So, she had a limited amount of time to reach her goal of securing a promotion. Radcliff, separated by many miles from his wife of over thirty years and his twin teen sons, was lonely and, therefore, susceptible to the wiles of the blonde beauty. Christy stopped short of seducing him (after all, he was older than her father), but she dangled the possibility of an affair before his hungry eyes like a honey-dipped carrot near the mouth of a starving rabbit.

The balding, bespectacled Radcliff was vulnerable and defenseless against the flattery Christy lavished upon him daily. She also expertly played the role of the hardworking but headache-prone Junior Officer, cajoling him into doing whatever she wanted. Thus, Christy sprang a trap that Radcliff unwittingly and happily stepped into. He allowed her to take doubly long lunch breaks, routinely arrive half an hour late, and leave the office early when she complained that she had *another* terrible migraine. The strategy paid off. After her first year at post, he gave her an annual performance evaluation of "Outstanding" and recommended her for a generous incentive cash award, which was forthcoming within a short time. He also recommended her for immediate promotion. The recommendation might or might not produce a sure thing as competitors at other posts would be vying for the limited number of promotions available, but Christy was optimistic. Radcliff's praise of her abilities exceeded even *her* expectations.

Nevertheless, what began as a seemingly ideal situation for Christy eventually gave rise to complications. First, Deputy Chief of Mission Sandra Charlemagne began patrolling the section each week, declaring that the staff had "a lot of catching up to do." The pressure on Radcliff to bring the section's backlog up-to-date was tremendous. He was relieved when Christy suggested that he request an additional local hire. She thought that would compensate for her own slack work ethic. He smilingly informed her that the request was "pending approval" and complimented her on her "brilliant" idea. Meanwhile, Christy's demands on her host-country subordinates fostered increased resentment against her, to which she was totally indifferent. The Colombian employees were earning more than they would get if they were employed outside the embassy, so (Christy concluded) they needed to stop their "whining."

The second complication was one that she couldn't ignore. Rod's deepening attraction to her was more than the usual male infatuation she was accustomed to dealing with. He was becoming obsessed with her. She felt as if she were being backed into a corner when he began hinting that she was more than just an employee to him. He confided that he had found a little cottage in a forested area outside the city that few, if any, of the embassy staff knew about. There, they could be completely alone together, away from prying eyes and wagging tongues. He had already rented it for the upcoming weekend. He would pick her up late Friday night, and they could be back in the city before midnight on Sunday.

Christy had to think fast. He was asking for more than she was willing to deliver, but she had to deliver *something* or risk having her scheme unravel. Oh, she might get the promotion, but working with Rod for another year could become unbearable. For she knew that sooner or later, *someone* would discover what was going on and report it to the Executive Office. *Wouldn't Sandra Charlemagne love to get a whiff of a scandal like that? The bloodhound!*

Christy entered Rod's Porsche that Friday night as pale as a white sheet (thanks to the clever application of makeup) with dark circles under her eyes. She was dressed in a short-sleeved white blouse that revealed a purplish bruise on one arm. Her flared red skirt reached just above her knees, one of which was wrapped in an elastic bandage. None of this was obvious until they reached the cottage, where Radcliff deposited their bags inside and eagerly switched on the entry door's light, which softly flooded the room in what he hoped was a romantic glow. Then, he gasped, taking in the starkly pitiful figure before him.

"Christy! What happened to you?"

"It's nothing really," she declared almost breathlessly. "I felt a migraine coming on last night, but I was running low on my pills, so I hurried down the stairs to drive to the pharmacy, and well, I ... I tripped and ... fell. Some kind lady noticed that my knee was bleeding and told the pharmacist to add the bandage and pills to her own bill. That was awfully nice of her, wasn't it? I managed to get what I needed -- that's what matters."

"My poor baby!" Radcliff crooned, leading her over to the loveseat. "I suppose you don't feel up to –" He left the suggestion hanging, and she appeared to make a brave effort at pleasing him.

"Not much, but we've been looking forward to this for *so* long that I wouldn't dream of letting a little pain spoil our special weekend together," she concluded with a wince that brought out his most solicitous mood.

"Nonsense, sweetheart! You just lie back and relax. I brought a bottle of champagne, and I'm going to fix dinner. I'm no chef, but –"

"Sweetie, I feel so useless lying here. Let me help," she offered in a faint tone as if the effort would bring on exhaustion.

"Next time, kitten, next time."

And that is how the weekend, for Radcliff, was ruined. Christy decided that, if necessary, she would invent another malady, and there would be no "next time."

By the time Radcliff dropped Christy off at her apartment, he had totally succumbed to her act of helplessness, and she was told to take the next two days off. He also insisted that she make an appointment with the embassy's Medical Officer for her bruises and migraines. She did, but canceled it two days before the appointment, opting instead to set up a private consultation. She knew that she couldn't hold Radcliff off for too much longer. She would have to devise a plan to cool his passion permanently by giving him a reason to believe he had a rival for her affections. That's why she chose a consultation with none other than the Colombian doctor she'd met at Sheila's party.

CHAPTER 14

Christy's attempts to secure an appointment with Diego Santos met with cool resistance on his part. His vocation was healing which, he realized, was not relevant to Christy Welles's case. Had he been a vain man, he might have been flattered by her persistent calls to the clinic, asking to speak with him, but he quickly recognized the signs of a woman with an ulterior motive. That motive was of no interest to him, and neither was she. There was only woman he was interested in: Sheila Dunbar. Therefore, when Christy appeared at the clinic a few days later, the receptionist, as per his instruction, informed her that he was unavailable. Christy then offered the pretext of needing contact information for a pain specialist, which the receptionist courteously provided. Grudgingly expressing gratitude, Christy took down the information, which she had no intention of ever using. Why would she? Migraines were a convenient ploy to get what she wanted, and she wanted Diego Santos, and not simply to ward off Rod's attentions. The fact that the handsome doctor was deliberately avoiding her made him even more desirable and as enticing as forbidden fruit.

Heretofore, other men had found Christy's beauty and charms irresistible; thus, like puppets, they could be manipulated to do her bidding. But the doctor apparently remained unmoved. Why? It couldn't be that he was actually attracted to *Sheila*! That little scene on Sheila's balcony at the party had been put on by the two for fun and dramatic effect. Whatever chemistry there had been between them couldn't have lasted beyond the party itself. Besides, she couldn't imagine any man taking a second look at Sheila when *she* was around. To Christy's way of thinking, Black women were the least appealing to the male eye. They were, in a word, *ugly*. So, who could blame their men for preferring women of other races, especially White women? Sheila Dunbar, she admitted, could be labeled *passable* in looks, but she was still undeniably Black and couldn't hold a man like Diego Santos. Christy's mind veered off into the possibility that they were involved more deeply than anyone at the embassy suspected, but the very idea rankled. No, she concluded, it hadn't gotten that far – not yet!

Christy was well aware that Sheila was one of many employees involved in advance preparations for a US Congressional Delegation (CODEL) visit, but her main concern was not the CODEL. She was more intrigued by the bouquet of flowers sent to Sheila at the embassy one morning. Christy had been in the lobby, greeting a Colombian visa applicant when a huge floral box arrived at the Marine Security Guard station, and she overheard the name of the intended recipient. She swiftly commandeered another Junior Officer to deal with the applicant and made her way up to the Political Section just in time to see the flowers placed on Sheila's desk. There was no mistaking the delight on her face as she opened the box and pulled back the tissue papers to reveal a card among the mound of pink blossoms.

Using the upcoming CODEL visit as her pretext, Christy chatted for a few minutes, finally commenting on the bouquet and leaning over to admire it. Sheila gingerly moved the box to the credenza behind her desk but not before Christy managed to read the card.

At that moment, Patrick Carmichael stepped out of his office and said, "Hi, Christy. What brings you to these parts?"

"Just curious to see how the other half operates," she joked with a giggle that sounded contrived, even to Pat.

"Welcome, welcome. It gets awfully lonely up here at the top," he sparred, tongue in cheek.

Having obtained the information she'd sought, she cited the call of duty and complimented Sheila on the "gorgeous" bouquet and the excellent taste of "whoever" the sender was.

On that note, Christy quickly returned to the Consular Section, mystified over what she had managed to glean from the card attached to Sheila's flowers: "In appreciation, Diego." The jealousy burning in her breast could only be extinguished in one way: capturing the man who, unlike all others, had eluded her *deliberately*. For any woman besides Christy, wounded pride would have been a deterrent against pursuing a man who was clearly uninterested, but Christy wasn't just any woman. Neither pride nor even self-respect factored into her emotions toward Diego Santos. The truth was that her vanity was deeply bruised, and it was a totally new experience for her. No man rejected Christy Welles — not if she could get him by eliminating her rival. However, there would be no confrontation. Oh no. That would smack too much of cattiness or, worse, attract sympathy to Sheila. Christy had another plan in mind, one that would smear the reputation of Ms. Goody Two-shoes for the rest of her career.

In the meantime, she had the annoying problem of Rod to deal with. Normally, she would have relished using him as a plaything to achieve her purposes, but Rod's infatuation was becoming ridiculous. He had learned of her visit to the Clínica Palermo and couldn't wait to question her. As she headed for her desk, Rod motioned for her to come into his office. Once inside, he closed the door and confronted her.

"Oh, Dr. Diego Santos? I went to the clinic to get some information about a pain specialist. I have the contact info in my purse if you want to see it."

Rod paused momentarily, then conceded, "That won't be necessary. I shouldn't be second-guessing you, but you know how I feel about you, Christy."

"I feel the same, Sweetie, so there's no reason to be jealous. Besides, the good doctor may already be spoken for. It seems I read of an engagement announcement a few months back."

"That didn't stop him from zeroing in on Sheila at the party."

Christy reluctantly nodded, then commented, "But Brad Davis might have something to say about that."

"Undoubtedly. He seemed completely bowled over by her. I hear he's back from Lima."

Rod then turned the conversation to his anticipation of another rendezvous with Christy. She was frustrated and barely managed to fake a credible amount of enthusiasm.

"Wonderful!" she cried, all the while mentally preparing her next strategy of escape from the net in which she had unwittingly become entangled.

****

While this was happening, Brad Davis, fresh from his temporary duty in Lima, Peru, appeared at Sheila's desk about an hour after Christy had left, eager to take up where they – or rather he – had left off. By then, the flowers had been placed in a dark-green crystal vase at one corner of the credenza, conspicuous by their abundance. Although Sheila had already slipped the card into her desk drawer, Brad wasted no time in finding out who the sender was.

"Nice flowers. Now, who could be trying to steal my girl?" he said, only half-jokingly.

"Dr. Santos sent them," Sheila replied in as casual a tone as she could summon.

Brad felt an almost surreal explosion of anger welling up inside him, but being the consummate professional that he was, he controlled himself and dropped a few well-rehearsed verbal charms before leaving. He probably would have laid them on much thicker if her boss hadn't persisted in hanging around her desk.

"My! Aren't you the popular one today?" Pat teased.

Sheila dryly commented, "It's the flowers. Have you smelled them? These pink roses aren't called 'Temptation' for nothing."

Pat laughed knowingly and departed for the latest Country Team meeting.

Sheila pulled out the card and fingered it, pondering if there might be a deeper meaning behind the message beneath the printed horticultural history of *la rosa Tentación*: "With appreciation, Diego."

No, she assured herself. She and Diego were just friends, but Christy probably believed otherwise. Brad probably thought so, too. Both of them would be surprised to learn that the appreciation expressed on the card was for nothing more than Sheila's agreement to partner with him in a Bible Q&A competition at the church. Six small teams of two to four players competed for the prize (a basket of tropical fruit), and Sheila's final answer clinched the win for her and Diego.

The phone rang. Answering in her usual cordial tone, Sheila was pleasantly surprised to hear Diego's voice at the other end of the line. It wasn't Wednesday, his day off, when she could normally expect a reminder about picking her up for the evening Bible study. It was Friday, and he was asking if she was free later that evening.

"Yes," she slowly responded.

He then asked her to have dinner with him. Once again, the word yes sounded hesitant and prolonged.

"Are you sure that you are available? You do not sound sure."

"I'm sure. It's just that – well, today is Friday. Thank you for the flowers by the way. The Q & A competition was fun, but that hardly calls for a celebration dinner – does it?"

"You are right, and we are not celebrating that win. We are celebrating you. Since I have to work next Monday, I was able to get this evening off. So, in advance, I wish you Happy Birthday, *amiga!*"

"How did you know?"

"I have my sources," he told her in soto voce fashion. "Shall I pick you up at seven?"

"Seven will be fine."

As she hung up the phone, her hand was shaking. Was this going to be a date? Of course, they had been on a few excursions: the Zipaquirá salt mine with its impressive little chapel; the Fusagasugá orchid farm; Villavicencio, a colonial town where she'd bought a warm green shawl; and the majestic Tequendama Falls. However, there had been nothing romantic about any of those outings. They'd simply been exploring like tourists, except she had been the tourist and he the tour guide. In fact, he'd always found a way to verbally insert a scripture relevant to the beauties of nature or history befitting whatever they were seeing.

Their conversations and many others never strayed beyond the limits of friendship. She knew that he was an engaged man. Although his was not a happy state, he and Sheila had an unspoken agreement to never cross into impropriety. That barrier must be maintained and respected. Why then, did she have the uneasy feeling that tonight might pose a challenge to their shared understanding? He had never before invited her to dinner, but it was her birthday. Perhaps he just wanted to do something special for a friend. *Friend*. Pushing an unwelcome thought out of her head, Sheila focused on the classified e-mails on her computer screen.

CHAPTER 15

Sheila soaked in a scented bath for half an hour in preparation for her outing with Diego. She was reluctant to think of it as a date because that hinted at an intimacy she knew she wasn't ready for. Ever since her divorce from Kevin's father, her priority had been raising her son, not becoming emotionally involved with another man. *But*, she told herself, *Kevin isn't* here now. Was she seeing too much of Diego, perhaps feeling lonely and trying to compensate for her son's absence? She couldn't afford to get too involved, yet she had to face the fact that she was already attracted to him. The image of the Latin wolf, her initial opinion of him, was contrary to who the man really was. Yes, he was handsome, but he was also kind, gentle, and principled – or so it seemed.

He could have hidden the fact that he was engaged – unhappily so – to the daughter of a wealthy businessman. He'd confided that his attempt to break the engagement had immediately preceded his father's heart attack. The wedding was postponed but not canceled. In light of his father's health, he felt powerless at this point to resolve the issue. Sheila suspected he was also carrying a load of guilt for his father's heart attack, although she had reasoned that it had probably not been precipitated by any action on Diego's part. Up until this invitation to dine with Diego tonight, she had not foreseen any problem with a platonic friendship. After all, her assignment here would be over in a matter of months. Then she would return to Washington, DC for home leave and, if necessary, language training at the Foreign Service Institute in preparation for wherever her next assignment would be.

She respected Diego for his honesty, but she wished that she could remain a little longer in Bogotá, even knowing that the relationship was going nowhere because he was still engaged.

Sheila applied her makeup sparingly, as usual, but experimented with her bulky hair, pulling it away from her face and pinning it into a French roll. Then she critically surveyed herself in the mirror. The new style emphasized the fine bone structure of her oval face and the slenderness of her neck. A crimson cashmere dress complemented her flawless complexion. It had been one of her rare splurges six years ago and still fit well. She was carefully arranging a fringed black shawl over her shoulders when the intercom buzzed to signal Diego's arrival. As she stepped off the elevator into the lobby, his look of admiration almost rocked her composure. She smiled and tried to ignore her racing heartbeats as he pinned scarlet-flecked cream orchids to the shoulder of her dress.

"Thank you. They're lovely," she said.

"So are you. You are wearing my favorite color," he commented, escorting her to his car and helping her in before sliding under the steering wheel.

He drove to Carrera Séptima, took a winding hill, and announced that they were on La Via Calera.

"This road leads to La Calera, a small town on the other side of those mountains. It has a lake for boating and a park. I must show it to you soon."

"I'd like that" Sheila politely responded, camouflaging her excitement at the prospect of another outing with him.

As they approached a thatch-roofed structure with enormous windows, all lit and glowing, she asked, "Is this Tramonti's?"

"Yes. Have you been here before?"

"No, but I've heard of it."

"I'm glad to be the first to show you the view from up here."

After declining pre-dinner drinks in the lower-level lounge, they were ushered up a flight of simple wooden stairs, past a roaring fireplace, to a table with a superb view of the city below. From this mountain vantage point, there were few other patrons that night. Sheila felt that she had entered some special and isolated world. The star-studded night sky stretched like an endless canopy over the sprawling valley with its myriad twinkling lights. The beauty of it took her breath away. Her eyes were luminous, her face a reflection of awe.

Diego smiled his pleasure and motioned for the waiter to bring the menu. They ate a delicious dinner of succulent, tender grilled steak; fresh spinach salad; rice pilaf; and shrimp in garlic butter, all washed down with single goblets of an excellent red wine. Little was said during the meal, as if the panorama below were too glorious to ruin with conversation. The whole night seemed to be touched with magic. From time to time, the two diners would glance up and speak a silent but eloquent message with their eyes – a message that seemed to say, "Tonight is ours to remember always."

Later, coffee was served, and a small Black Forest cake with a single candle was placed at the center of the table. She blew out the candle as Diego sang the Spanish version of "Happy Birthday."

Finally, the bill was paid. The waiter bestowed a red rose on Sheila, a customary gesture toward women diners. Then, they were winding their way back down the mountainside, she thanking him for a wonderful evening, he assuring her that the pleasure had been his.

On arriving at her apartment, he extracted the keys from her fumbling fingers and unlocked the door. Inside, he offered to build a fire for her, commenting, "These Andean nights can be quite chilly."

"I'm not cold. Are you?"

"No, no," he quickly replied.

They stood in the living room, awkwardly facing each other. Diego's hands were shoved so deeply into his trouser pockets that his knuckles strained against the fabric.

"Won't you sit down?" Sheila offered.

Slightly hitching his trousers, he sat down in the stuffed chair adjacent to the sofa and placed an ankle over the top of one knee.

"Would – would you care for something to drink?" she ventured, nervously wringing her hands.

"Water, if you please," he said.

She hurried to the kitchen; poured a glass of iced water; inhaled deeply; and sailed back into the living room, no more composed than when she had left it. She dropped down onto the sofa, clenching her hands in her lap. Silence hung heavily between them for several moments, neither meeting the other's eyes. Diego slowly sipped the water and surveyed the toe of his highly polished shoe.

What are we afraid of? Sheila asked herself. They had never been so tense in each other's presence before. Yet there was something different about tonight. What was it? She looked up. He was still staring at the toe of his shoe.

"It was a beautiful evening, Diego. I'll never forget it," she remarked with quiet sincerity.

"Neither will I," he responded, his eyes so eloquent that she could not mistake his meaning.

The next moment, he was beside her on the sofa, clasping her hands in his and gazing into her face with a longing that left her speechless, but only for a second.

"Yes, it was quite an evening. What a view!" she exclaimed, withdrawing her hands and moving away from the sofa to stall for time. Time to come to grips with what she had seen in his eyes. What she had both secretly hoped for and dreaded would happen *had* happened, and she didn't know how to deal with it.

Knowing full well that he was engaged, albeit unhappily, to another woman hadn't stopped her from trying to convince herself that their relationship was harmless. He had been truthful with her early on about the engagement. He'd confided how guilty he felt about arguing with his father and perhaps precipitating the heart attack. The postponement of the wedding had strained the relationship between father and son even further.

Their no-strings-attached arrangement had been working fine – or so she'd assumed. They had been on only a few outings besides seeing each other at the weekly Bogotá Baptist Chapel Bible studies on Wednesday nights. On Sundays, they attended their respective churches, she in the mornings, he in the evenings, explaining that on Sunday mornings, he was often on call at the clinic. Gradually, she became aware that she had begun to look forward to Wednesdays more than Sundays. Tonight, she realized that their friendship was evolving into something deeper and perhaps bigger than she could handle. She had been living in a fool's paradise, telling herself that what they had was mere friendship. If only he weren't so likable, so lovable. If only he -

Sheila was given no more time for reflection. Diego's hands were on her shoulders, turning her around to face him. A gentle finger nudged her chin up, and she met his eyes, so full of tenderness that she couldn't look away. His tone was low, ardent.

"I love you, Sheila. *¡Te amo tanto!*"

"Well, do you love me enough to never see me again – for the good of us both?"

"What?" he asked, stunned.

"You heard me," Sheila said.

"Please, don't do this," he whispered. "You are ripping me apart!"

"Spare me," Sheila said in a cynical tone. "You're getting married –"

"No! I won't marry Rosa. I do not love her, and I told my father so. Believe me, I will find a way out of this mess, and then –"

"And then what? You told me that you're not afraid of your father's threat to ruin your career. What if it's not just a scare tactic? Are you willing to take that risk, Diego? That would be a heavy price to pay for another six months."

"Six months? What do you mean?"

"The end of my assignment. Surely you realize that *whatever* we have here is temporary, that it's just –"

"Sh!" he interrupted, placing a finger over her lips. "I want more, much more, and I promise you, *mi vida,* that if you are as willing as I, we can make this work. Promise me that you will think about it."

"Diego, I can't promise you anything – not as long as you're engaged. I shouldn't have let it get this far. I think it's best if we don't see each other anymore."

"Sheila, do not say it is over when we have hardly begun. What about the Wednesday night Bible studies? Even if I don't pick you up, we still would see each other there."

"I won't be attending the studies anymore."

"You are *that* determined to avoid me," he commented with a dejected sigh.

"It's the only way, Diego. You could end up married. I could never be the other woman."

"And I would never expect you to be. Trust me. I will find a way," he said, raking a hand through his hair and beginning to pace the floor before suddenly halting before her. "There is a way! You need not stop attending the studies, and you could keep me current on the discussions. We could have our own study each week by telephone!"

He sounded almost desperate, and it wrenched her conscience. She *would* miss him. Besides, as long as their calls didn't become personal, what harm would there be? Or might she be setting herself up for heartache later on, knowing the pull he already had on her emotions?

"It – it might work. Just remember that it's the Bible we'll be discussing – nothing more," she said, trying to inject a toughness into her tone that she was far from feeling.

"I will remember," Diego said solemnly, pulling her into his arms for a moment – a moment that seemed all too brief to Sheila. As if resisting some mesmerizing force, he dragged his gaze from her face to the floor, then held her aloof before quickly turning away. A few seconds later, the door closed behind him with a soft click. Sheila felt a terrible emptiness as tears slowly coursed down her cheeks.

CHAPTER 16

That should have made life easier for Sheila: putting some physical distance between herself and a man that she might not ever be able to call her own. Yet she couldn't think of Diego without wishing things were different. But, of course, wishing changed nothing. He was still engaged to be married. She supposed she should be satisfied with the few verbal crumbs she devoured when he called for an update of the weekly Wednesday night Bible studies at the chapel. The truth was that between those calls, she counted the days, sometimes even the hours until the next phone call. And those calls, as benign as they seemed, stirred her as nothing else could. The mere sound of his voice thrilled her, tempted her to prolong their discussions, veer off into other topics – off-limit topics about the status of his relationships with his father and his fiancée. Worse, she longed for more than a phone call. She wanted to see his face, experience once more the quickening of her heartbeats at his embrace, however brief, or the gentle touch of his finger beneath her chin. Sensibly, she forced a neutrality, almost a detachment into her voice each time they talked. And Diego, being a man of his word, remained cordial and cool, remembering that they were to discuss only the

Bible, and always ending their calls with *Dios te bendiga* – God bless you.

This evening, Sheila was reviewing a half-dozen Post Reports on the side table next to her sofa. They were related to the six choices she had listed for her next assignment, ranking them numerically to indicate her preferences. Having willingly chosen Bogotá, a dangerous and "hardship" post (due to several factors, including the high altitude), she knew that there was a good chance of her getting her first or second choice. Her options were Mexico City, Paris, La Paz, Seoul, Tokyo and Zagreb.

 She had thought long and hard about the possibility of placing Timbuktu, Mali at the top of her list. In ancient times, Mali was a great center of education and rich culture, a glorious kingdom which inspired stories of daring adventures. Cynthia Nelson, the Ambassador's personal assistant, had begun her Foreign Service career there. In fact, Cynthia had given her a box covered in camel skin from Mali. From Cynthia and the *Post Report,* Sheila learned that Mali's days of glory were long over. Timbuktu was now another "hardship" post, however fascinating its history, or regardless of its remaining culture and craftsmanship. Those alone might be worth a tour of duty there. She sighed in regret. She was kidding herself! Her mother would never sanction her taking Kevin there. As much as Sheila wanted an African assignment, she had to be level-headed, not selfish, about this. Well, her mother wouldn't object to the preferences she'd listed. The deadline to submit them to State Department headquarters was another week.

Her thoughts wandered back to Diego.

"Oh, no!" she lamented.

She tried to concentrate on their Bible discussion series titled "His Grace Is Sufficient", but her thoughts kept returning to the familiar dangers: buses overturned and burned; private security guards being shot down at the residences of prominent citizens; kidnappings of investigative journalists, activists, dissidents, American missionaries, etc. Not all her insomnia was edged with worry for herself alone but also for Diego; for she knew that as the son of a wealthy businessman, he too might become a target of kidnappers or, worse, assassins. It was during those times that she would play soft inspirational music or open her Bible to seek serenity from certain psalms, most often Psalm 91, verse 1: "He who dwells in the secret place of the Most High shall abide under the shadow of the Almighty" *(NKJV).* Then, she would drift off to sleep only to awaken much too early and begin thinking of Diego again.

Another security-focused memorandum had just been updated and was circulating among the embassy staff. It reiterated the same regulations, but this time it also reported the injury suffered by a young US Marine in the front lobby at the hands of an irate visa applicant. He had intervened when she lunged for the Junior Officer who was interviewing her. While the Junior Officer escaped unscathed, the Marine's face bore glaring evidence of the attack. The woman had slapped and raked his face with her long fingernails before he subdued her and had one of the Colombian guards expel her from embassy premises. Visitors' weapons were always confiscated, but who could have predicted such a vicious assault from an unarmed person?

What would the RSO say if he knew that she hadn't been adhering to all the precautions and restrictions "set in stone"? She always drove to Wednesday night Bible studies, varying her routes each time, but on Sundays she occasionally rode the bus to morning services at the chapel – clearly forbidden, and for good reason. Just a month ago, she had disembarked from the bus and was almost at her apartment building three blocks away when a bomb exploded at the bank near the bus stop. The explosion shook the entire area, killing a woman walking past the bank. But for the passage of several minutes, she too would have been a victim of the bombing.

Then there was what happened last Wednesday night. She had followed the rules (well, most of them) and *still* had fallen prey to a taxi driver who was clearly unhinged. She'd decided not to drive to the Bible study but to take a taxi. Perfectly allowable provided certain precautions were taken: agreeing on the fare before entering the taxi; wearing no obvious US insignia (tee-shirts, caps); minimizing conversation with the driver; keeping your security radio with you (concealed, of course); and never, ever admitting where you were from. In any case, having agreed on the fare prior to entering the taxi, the first alarm bell went off in Sheila's head at the first red traffic light. The driver quoted a higher fare amount. Thinking that the smart thing to do was to agree, she nodded and said, "Sí, señor." However, it soon became apparent that her assent hadn't settled the matter. As the light turned green, he sped up and demanded another higher payment. Agreeing again, Sheila realized that his demands weren't likely to stop with that amount. As he halted at another traffic light, she reached for the door handle. To her horror, her hand met a flat panel devoid of any handle. Fumbling around in the dark, she discovered a handle near the floor and tugged – to no avail. The door was locked and obviously controlled by the driver from some mechanism in the front. A low chuckle told her that the driver was aware of her futile effort to escape. She slumped back against her seat, the pounding in her ears signaling a panic that threatened to snuff out all rational thought. Slowly, she inhaled and exhaled, trying to calm herself. The driver certainly must be aware of her nervousness and on guard against any sudden moves she might make. But what *could* she do, trapped in a cab with a driver intent on – what? He briefly turned on the ceiling light, long enough to light a tan cigarette and for Sheila to catch a glimpse of steely eyes and a malevolently sneering mouth.

The taxi was leaving the boulevard, slowing down, and entering an area with fewer lights. The road gave her a clue that this was not the way to the church. Its surface was uneven, bumpy. Off in the distance, she could see tall buildings, lit apartments and business offices. Closer to where they were now, houses – one- and two-story residences with red-tiled roofs – were visible. The driver switched off the interior light and pulled onto a huge, dark, empty field enclosed on three sides by brick walls. At the open entry was a luminescent sign announcing upcoming construction. Please, God. No! She had to get out – now! As if the driver had read her thoughts, he chuckled again and began to slowly circle the field, his low-beam headlights guiding him along its perimeter.

"¿Qué quiere, señor?" *What do you want, sir?* Her question was soft, respectful

"Verás," he responded. You'll see.

Her throat tightened, but she managed to croak out, "Por favor, señor, si el dinero es lo que quiere –" *Please, sir, if it's money that you want –*

"El dinero – y más," he commented, barely above a whisper. *The money – and more.*

Her thoughts were now in a desperate tailspin. Money she had: five hundred pesos that she was going to – or had intended to contribute to a new mission, Servants of the King, that the church was supporting. She dreaded the "más," trying to stave off a woman's worst fears. He could have all the money; his getting more was the dilemma. He wouldn't if she could prevent it. She must!

"¿De dónde eres?" *Where are you from?*

Her vague response of "África" seemed to put him in a lyrical mood.

"África," he remarked with relish. "¡Ay! A mí me gusta el chocolate caliente y dulce."

So, he liked hot, sweet chocolate? She replied in Spanish that she also liked chocolate, especially with her Colombian coffee. When he threw back his head in uproarious laughter, she cringed. Instead of matching his wit with her own, she feared that her words might provoke him into some act of aggression, which she hoped to avoid long enough to escape.

He brought the taxi to an abrupt, rocking halt and, releasing the rear door lock, he gruffly ordered her out.

As Sheila stumbled from the back seat, she noticed that the taxi's low-beamed lights were still on. She dashed behind the taxi, but he quickly overtook her, dragging her toward a brick wall, but not before she had seen and memorized the lit license plate number. He warned her not to even *think* of escaping. Pain shot through her wrist as he tightened his grip. When she kept struggling, he commanded, "¡Pare!" *Stop*! Trying to twist out of his grasp was useless, and she suddenly froze when he jerked her to his chest and pressed the blade of a knife to her throat. In terror she squeezed her eyes shut, her pulses racing as she silently prayed, *Help me, Oh, God, please help me!* Moving the tip of the blade along the base of her left jaw, he whispered that his name was Juan. When he asked hers and she didn't answer, he growled in frustration, then remarked that it didn't matter because when it was all over, both of them would be satisfied.

Satisfied? The man must be a lunatic, a raving lunatic! Only God could rescue her now – God and, if she could pull it off, the element of surprise.

"A las rodillas." *On your knees.* The order was cold and menacing.

Sheila rubbed her aching wrist and slowly sank to the ground. Her relief was almost palpable as he took the knife away from her jaw and placed it into the sheath at his hip. Her relief, however, was momentary as he began unbuckling his belt while ordering her to lie on her back and relax. *Relax? No, this can't be happening!* She leaned back and, in the flash of a split-second, an anguished cry issued from her throat as her jutting right foot lifted up in a hard kick, brutally connecting with his crotch. Scrambling to her feet, she fled toward the construction sign at the entrance. Loud thudding sounded in her ears. She looked back, afraid of being overtaken, but "Juan" was in no condition to pursue her. He was on the ground, his bent form barely visible in the night shadows as his livid curses punctured the chilly air. She sprinted out of the field, clutching her handbag to her chest.

 As the boulevard gradually came into view, she slowed to a brisk walk. Winded and exhausted, she was terrified that he might quickly recover and come after her. She lost track of time as she trudged on, relying on her recall of certain signs and intersections. And all the while, she kept repeating the license plate number in her head. Eventually, she recognized her own neighborhood and pushed ahead, her breath coming in gasps. Had it been hours since she'd left the taxi driver in the field, shouting obscenities at the indignity of her assault? No, not hours. Otherwise, she couldn't have come this far already. She saw the green space across from her multi-story building and resumed running again, rushing up the steps and pressing the bell in a prolonged peal. The doorman hurried forward to open the front door, doffing his cap. She must have looked a mess because his eyes widened as he asked if she was alright. She murmured that of course she was. He summoned the elevator, still staring as she stepped inside and began the ascent to her apartment.

At her door, her hands were shaking so much that she could hardly fit the key into the lock. Once inside, she took a pen and pad from her purse and wrote down the memorized license plate number. Her legs almost gave way before she reached her living room sofa and collapsed, the reality of what she'd endured totally engulfing her senses.

CHAPTER 17

The next day was Thursday. Sheila got up from the sofa. *The sofa?* Had she spent the night on the sofa? Why? Then it all came rushing back to her! She must have blacked out last night. Resolutely, she pushed the events of the previous night away; padded into the bathroom to get ready for work, then hurried down to the lobby to await her ride to the embassy. Through the lobby's plate-glass door, she saw a group of poor kids gathering on the steps. Her initial generosity to one little boy brought more children in increasing numbers. These days she quickly dropped a few coins into one palm, the one nearest the door, before dashing to the embassy van. Today was no different.

Following its random schedule, the van arrived forty-five minutes later than it had on Wednesday. As usual, an armed guard jumped out of the chase car; ran up the front steps; escorted her from the lobby to the van; then hopped back into the chase car before signaling the van's chauffeur to proceed to the next pick-up. After the final pick-up, the van would proceed, as usual, to the embassy by a circuitous route. As the van moved away from her building, Sheila noticed that the small recipient of her coins had managed to break away from his companions and was outdistancing them as they took chase. *Go, go, go!* she silently cheered him on as he rounded a corner, disappearing from sight.

The traffic seemed heavier and more chaotic today, Sheila thought – or was it her imagination? She sat in stoic silence, hardly aware of her fellow passengers, her nerves on edge, until both vehicles cleared the checkpoint for bombs and were admitted through the high, iron gate before rolling into the embassy's only parking lot behind the chancery. For the first time since arriving for duty in Bogotá, she noticed the number of guards stationed all around the iron fencing. Were there really over a hundred of them, not including those that manned the front ramp and main entry? Then there was the US Marine Security Guard Detachment responsible for the lobby. An urgent tap on her shoulder startled her. The young Colombian bodyguard nicknamed "Pepe" snapped, "¡Rápido!" *Quickly!* Sheila blinked and apologized, knowing that her distraction could endanger not only herself but also others. Yet, up until today, she hadn't fully absorbed that fact. If she had, she wouldn't have taken such a cavalier attitude about the rules. She sometimes rode in buses and, except at work, she never kept her radio with her, blatant violations of embassy regulations. However, it was a good thing that her radio wasn't with her last night. "Juan" might have discovered it, confiscated or destroyed it. Worse, he might have used it to monitor embassy communications, although unclassified over public airwaves. This morning, she would report the incident and, necessarily, explain why she hadn't used her radio to call for help.

Pat accompanied her to the RSO where she handed over a written memorandum detailing the incident, including an admission that she'd left her radio in her apartment and offering what she hoped was a plausible explanation for doing so. (It didn't fit into the purse she was carrying.) Witt Jones wasn't buying it. He briefly reprimanded her and then began the lengthy interrogation. He elicited every single detail that she could recall: a description of the exterior and interior of the vehicle; what the abductor looked like (his age, height, weight, hair texture and color, eye color, skin tone, facial features, distinguishing marks like moles, scars, tattoos); what he was wearing; his speech pattern; the weapon; the location and its surroundings. On and on, Jones probed, sounding almost disinterested, as if he'd conducted thousands of interrogations as a matter of routine — which he probably had. He informed Sheila that the driver's stated first name of "Juan" was so common that it would be of no assistance, but when she provided the taxi's license plate number, his interest peaked. After reading the memo a second time and reviewing all that she'd said, Jones asked if she'd noticed anything else distinctive about "Juan" like missing teeth.

"No. It was dark, but he did briefly turn on a light to get a hand-rolled cigarette. I didn't notice anything unusual about his face — just his, his cold eyes and — and cruel mouth," Sheila said with an involuntary shudder.

Pat intervened at that point.

"Witt, I think you've gotten just about all you can for the moment."

"Yeah," Jones said with a curt nod, then added, "That'll do — for now, Sheila. If you think of anything else, even the smallest detail not mentioned this morning, don't hesitate to call us. Meanwhile, we'll run a check on that license plate with DAS —

the Colombian Administrative Department of Security. Are you sure about the number?"

"Yes. I memorized it, repeated it in my head, and wrote it down once I got back to my apartment."

"Good," Jones said, dismissing her and Pat with another nod before disappearing into his office.

Back in the Political Section, Pat commented, "Sheila, I won't ask the real reason why you thought it was okay to skirt the rules. Not having the radio with you last night was probably fortunate, but going forward, I'm warning you not to play fast and loose with your safety and, frankly, that of the rest of us. There. I've had my say. What have you to say in defense of your behavior?"

"Nothing, Pat. My behavior was indefensible," Sheila quietly responded.

Pat suggested that considering the ordeal she'd been through, she might want to take the rest of the day off."

"That's generous of you, Pat. I'll leave an hour early today."

* *

Sheila was seated in the security van, glancing through the side window at the rapidly moving traffic when something caught the corner of her eye, something she had not noticed before. Just above the lower rim of the window's stripping were two bullets. Bullets that had penetrated but not passed through the van's ballistic glass shield.

The embassy had a fleet of vans. This perhaps was not the same van that she had ridden to work in this morning; however, it was the same model and was outfitted for security like all the other vans in the fleet. She wondered when the van had been shot at. Had other vans in the fleet come under fire? These were questions she had no intention of asking. She really didn't want to know the answers. Since the embassy's security-related bulletins failed to mention any such incident, perhaps even the RSO was clueless.

CHAPTER 18

The persistent ringing of the telephone jarred Sheila from her lethargy. It was nine p.m. on Thursday evening, the time when Diego usually went off duty at the clinic and called for an update on the Bible study at the chapel.

"Diego, good evening. How are you?"

"I am fine, Sheila, but you are not. Pastor Pittman said you were not at the Bible study last night."

"That's right. I didn't make it."

"Why? No, do not answer. I'm coming there, Sheila," he said.

"Diego –"

The phone's dial tone signaled that he'd hung up. Fifteen minutes later, the doorman announced his arrival. By then, Sheila had washed her face, applied light makeup, and put on a clean blouse. The doorbell rang. As she opened the door, Diego pulled her into his arms and she silently clung to him, finding comfort in his embrace. Finally, she stepped away from him and led him into the living room where he joined her on the sofa.

"I tried to reach you for more than an hour. I was worried. I *am* worried. Tell me what has happened, Sheila. Are you not feeling well?"

"No, it's nothing like that."

"Then, tell me."

"Diego, we had an agreement…not to see each other until –"

"Forget the agreement. Your well-being is much more important than the debacle I find myself in right now. So, let us, as they say, 'cut to the chase'."

When she hesitated, he took both her hands in his. They were cold. He stood up, walked over to the fireplace, and restarted the fire. When he returned to her side, her hands were covering her face. He gently pulled them down and tilted her chin up softly to ask, "Do you trust me?"

"Yes, I do," she responded.

"Then, tell me what happened, *mi amor*."

Was she truly his love? That was her undoing. She fell against his shoulder, sobbing. Once again, his arms closed around her, and she didn't want the embrace to end but, after composing herself, she told him what happened the previous night.

"The miserable coward!" he exclaimed. "How dared he touch you!"

"Well, it's over now," she said with relief.

"We can only hope so," Diego commented.

"You don't think … he'll try to find me?" Sheila asked with bated breath.

"I do not know, but the humiliation of an assault, although deserved, on his … manhood might motivate him to look for you."

"No!" Sheila whispered.

"Do not fear. I will do all I can to protect you."

"I appreciate that, but you can't be with me twenty-four seven."

"True, but you can become much less visible. You have protection to, at, and from the embassy. It is away from the embassy that you may be vulnerable. Your maid still comes to clean?"

Sheila nodded.

"What about the grocery shopping?"

"She usually does that too."

"If ever she is not available or you need extra help, I can call Lucy. Yes?"

"Okay," she said.

"The coward may return to the area where he picked you up in the hope of spotting you. So, no taxis, no buses, no driving your car, no –"

"Wait. Next, you'll be saying no church attendance. I *won't* become a hermit."

"You will not have to. I will pick you up for the Bible study on Wednesday nights. Remain in the garage until I signal twice with my car horn. Agreed?"

"Agreed. And Sunday mornings?"

"I will request a change in my work schedule. Then I can accompany you to your Sunday morning services and still keep attending my church on Sunday evenings."

"What if the change isn't granted?" Sheila asked.

"It will be," he firmly answered, then ventured, "Perhaps you would like to accompany me next Sunday evening? The Continental Singers will be in concert on behalf of a charity called 'Save the Children.' Have you heard them?"

"No, but I'm familiar with the charity. I'm already looking forward to it," Sheila said with a smile.

"So am I," Diego said with an answering smile, adding, "For more reasons than one."

Sheila lay her head on his shoulder and sighed in contentment for several wordless minutes. Slowly, he released her but kept her hand in his as she walked him to the door.

"Sleep well," he whispered with an adoring gaze before leaving.

CHAPTER 19

The taxi's license plate number was registered to a known member of the M-19. All the more reason that Sheila worried about "Juan" finding her. The embassy would keep the data on the incident in its security files but, other than reminding her to be extra careful, nothing would be done unless DAS chose to do it, and the Colombians had their hands full. Their nation was under siege. In the weeks that followed, print and broadcast media reported the death of Ivan Marino, a well-known terrorist, as well as more victims of M-19 and FARC (Colombian Revolutionary Forces). Activists and Catholic priests in rural and urban areas who dared speak out against drug lords or guerillas met violent and untimely deaths. An American missionary group lost a member when ransom demands were not met. A DEA informant had been missing for several weeks, and one of their Special Agents was gravely wounded at a local café, presumably because he let down his guard, becoming an easy target.

Sheila tossed the latest daily edition of "El Tiempo" aside, trying to mentally erase the front-page image of Ivan Marino's dead face, photographed as a close-up after a gruesome take-down by Colombian law enforcement.

Once again, staff were confined to the embassy chancery during the lunch hour. She missed her forays to the park on Séptima Avenue but dared not defy the rules again.

"Can you believe the latest attack?" Pat commented.

"I know. It's sad, but it could have been worse. Agent Packard had a close call. With all the rehab, he won't be certified for duty again for at least another year – if ever. I'm sure his wife and kids are grateful that his tour here is being curtailed."

"Well, DEA is tightening its security even more, so his replacement should feel a bit safer."

"As always, the show – or rather the work – must go on," Sheila said. She herself was beginning to feel the strain.

Diego *had* been able to get his Sundays off and, apart from his regular Wednesdays, Sheila welcomed his nightly telephone calls to check on her. The subject of his engagement was deliberately avoided, and Sheila knew that nothing had been resolved. *So far*, she mentally added, trying to keep hope alive. Theirs was an unspoken bond, a mutual attraction which had to remain platonic, at least on the surface.

She surveyed the amount of work on her desk - *so much for going paperless* – and resigned herself to getting home late again.

From time to time, her mind wandered to the locally hired Colombian staff. Without their expertise and many services, the embassy would lack the continuity and stability that all diplomatic missions required to function efficiently. For the FSNs (Foreign Service Nationals) were essential to the embassy's smooth operation (barring the handling of classified data, which they had no access to).

In such a class-conscious society, however, it was often difficult to distinguish the Colombian personnel from the US diplomatic staff. In fact, one of the maintenance men, Pablo Montoya, dressed with as much finesse as the Ambassador himself. Every weekday, a perfectly groomed Pablo arrived in a pinstripe navy or gray suit, white shirt with burgundy "silk" tie and silver-tone cufflinks. His black loafers wore a spotless shine, and he carried a handsome briefcase of oxblood leather. Inside the briefcase were his work shoes and uniform. A quick change in the restroom readied him for duty. At day's end, Pablo the businessman emerged and once again presented his professional image to Colombian society. To Sheila's amazement, the char force ladies followed the same practice – arriving in nice dresses and dark pumps, while presenting a flawless appearance with their stylish hair-dos, carefully applied makeup, and jewel-hued manicured nails. Sheila glanced at her own short fingernails coated in clear polish. Well, she couldn't very well type with long nails, could she? Besides, tinted nails were not as easy to maintain.

The day indeed was long. It was after seven when she finally locked up and headed toward the rear basement door to catch a security van home. At the elevator stood Elton Wilkes, the tall, trim young office manager of the ECON Section. His blond hair, blue eyes, and fair complexion were features that the average Colombian associated with foreigners, visitors from "Gringolandia."

"Hi, cutie pie," he said in a languid southern drawl.

"Elton, isn't it past your bedtime?" Sheila teased.

"Not tonight. Sweetwater had me sending out faxes – although *he* left on time."

The elevator opened, and they stepped inside. Not surprisingly, they were the only employees still here (apart from Cynthia Nelson who routinely worked late for the Ambassador). As the security van pulled out of the parking lot, they talked about their preferences for their next assignments.

"I hear the ECON Section in Madrid has an opening."

"True, but I placed it last on my preference list."

"Why?"

"Bangkok is more my cup of tea. Lots of gorgeous guys there, I hear."

"That wouldn't be your *only* motivation for wanting to go there, would it?" Sheila asked.

"Oh, wouldn't it," Elton stated matter-of-factly. "What about you?"

"I'm listing Mexico City as my top choice."

"You go, girl! You've earned it and deserve a better gig. We all do (except a certain you-know-who in the Consular Section).

"Well, the Colombian staff isn't going anywhere. If they can endure this chaos and violence, why should we complain?"

"Because we can," Elton said with a shrug.

The conversation turned to the latest news among the staff.

"Say, Elton, you're not hopping on the cosmetic surgery bandwagon, are you?"

"If I do, I'll have to take a number and get in line. Girl, I *am* tempted. I have a reference for a great laser eye surgeon. These US-trained Colombian doctors charge a fraction of what we pay in the States."

"And apparently produce outstanding results. Have you noticed the Agricultural Attaché's wife lately?"

"Everybody's noticed. The difference is amazing – and was badly needed."

"Yes, *all* those pockmarks on her face – gone!"

"Well, it was smart of Colleen to take advantage of the procedure before they leave post. The Kellers are retiring to their hometown in East Texas – Beaumont, I believe."

"I've heard of it. The folks there are in for a big surprise," Sheila said.

"Speaking of surprises, the latest on the pipeline hit us like a cyclone."

"Another good name being dragged through the muddy rumor mill?" Sheila asked.

"No rumor this time. Honey, you could have knocked me over with a feather, as we say in my old neck of the woods. Tabby –"

Sheila nudged Elton with her elbow, and he fell silent. She changed the subject.

"It's too bad that Frank Ferguson couldn't finish his temporary duty here."

"A crying shame," Elton commented. "He had passed all his tests before coming. Well, we're not getting hardship pay for nothing."

"The thin air at this high altitude has taken down a few TDYers," Sheila said.

"I wish it hadn't been Frank," Elton noted before adding, "Did you see those biceps?"

They were arriving at his apartment building, so Sheila was spared the need to make more small talk. The armed chauffeur escorted Elton to the lobby entrance where the doorman was waiting to quickly admit him.

Next, Sheila was dropped off and rushed into her building. She paused to catch her breath as the uniformed doorman summoned the elevator.

A few minutes later, she kicked off her shoes, flopped down onto her sofa, and began sipping a cup of hot, spiced cinnamon tea. Massaging her temples with her fingertips, she mulled over Elton's penchant for chatter – and how much she would miss it once this assignment was over. For unlike some staff, his chatter never evolved into malicious gossip. Why then had she cut him off when he was going to talk about Tabitha "Tabby" Sands? She surely couldn't be jealous of the forty-four-year-old Personnel Officer marrying one of the embassy chauffeurs, a man twenty years her junior, during a quick trip to Miami. After all, the entire staff knew the gritty details surrounding the whirlwind courtship and union, as well as the common opinion that the groom had married her specifically to obtain a green card. Besides, she herself had no reason to be jealous of anyone. She was focused on completing this assignment and getting back to DC. She was a career woman, but her first priority was to her son. *Why, then, are you spending more and more of your evenings speculating about Diego's engagement?*

"I am *not* speculating!" she spoke the words aloud, then clamped her hand over her mouth in amazement.

She may as well admit that the stagnant situation between her and Diego was a persistent cause for – what? Concern? Yes. Hopelessness? No, not that she would admit it at this point.

The talk about matrimony was a sensitive barb that irritated her regardless of who was involved. Was it too much to hope for a resolution (more like a dissolution) of Diego's engagement? Then what?

Snap out of it! she chided herself. And she did – when the telephone rang and the warm, inviting tone at the other end of the line lifted her out of her doldrums. It was Diego.

CHAPTER 20

I t was Wednesday night. Sheila barely had time to get home from the office, take a quick shower, and prepare to be picked up by Diego. These days she never drove her car, so she slipped a key into her MG's ignition to keep the battery activated. This was done as she waited in the basement garage, listening for the double toot of the Mustang's horn – a signal that it was safe to leave the garage. However, tonight, no signal came. It was fifteen minutes past the time that Diego usually arrived. What was delaying him? Surely not duty at the clinic; this was his day off. She again checked the luminous face of her wristwatch. If he didn't get here soon, they'd be late for the Bible study. Another ten minutes passed. She was thinking of going upstairs to call his private number when a prolonged honk from a car horn sounded. She must have somehow missed his first signal. Even so, it wasn't like him to be impatient. After all, *she* wasn't the one who was late. Opening the side door of the garage, she dashed outside and into almost blinding headlights. Diego usually waited until she was inside his car to turn on the headlights. Why hadn't he done so tonight? She ran over to the front passenger door, snatched it open, and gasped as her eyes alighted on an empty driver's seat. The alarm in her brain came too late as a low cackle sounded from behind her and a beefy hand closed over her mouth and nose. A sepulchral whisper reminded her that his name was "Juan." She assumed that he was going to try to push her into the back seat of what she now realized was his taxi. Instead, he began dragging her backwards toward a huge shrub leaning against the brick wall of the building. If he got her behind that bush, no one would see them. She tried to twist her head from side to side, but his grip on her face was like an iron vice, and he tightened it to the point that she felt almost smothered. With a jerking motion, he warned her to be still or he would break her neck. To reinforce the threat, he unsheathed his knife with his free hand and pressed the tip of its blade against her neck. In a guttural tone, he added that he was not in the mood for games and, indeed, the time had come for *la venganza*, payback.

At that moment, a voice whispered, "I will never leave you nor forsake you." She had no time to analyze from which direction it had come or if it had only been a thought, but a peace flooded her inner being and banished her fear. She remembered that she was carrying not only her handbag but, in a deep pocket of her skirt, her embassy radio, which was turned off. What if Juan discovered it? Well, not if she could help it! He laughed again, that unholy cackle which had sent a chill up her spine a moment ago but now only annoyed her. He probably assumed that she was as helpless as a bird caught in his net. For he began addressing her as his *palomita* (little dove). She did feel helpless when the radio fell out of her skirt pocket, clattering to the asphalt just as they reached the shrub. The sudden distraction caused Juan to loosen his grip and turn to seek the source of the noise. *Now!* Sheila wrenched herself free and fled down the sloped driveway screaming for help. "*¡Ayúdeme!*" The headlights of another car caught them both in its arc as Juan chased and, reaching out, grabbed her wrist. His knife flashed toward her face and connected with her left jaw. The squeal of the other car's tires rent the night air as the driver braked, but that didn't stop Juan from pulling Sheila back up the driveway toward the shrub, fiercely determined despite her resistance. A curse exploded from his lips, a threat that he would kill her if she kept struggling. But fast footfalls and an overpowering presence behind him cut short any further threat. A heavy blow to his head caused the culprit to release his hold on her, fall to his knees, and roll to the side of the driveway, face-up and still.

The man brusquely ordered her to come with him. Stunned, Sheila stood there immobile with wide, incredulous eyes. Had she been abducted by one man only to become the victim of the one who had rescued her – if indeed this was a rescue? It didn't make sense.

"Sheila, *mi amor*, come!"

Her name and the endearment propelled her into Diego's arms. At the top of the slope, Sheila pulled away from him.

"My radio, my embassy radio! It fell out."

"We will find it," he reassured her.

Diego extracted a small penlight from his jacket. Following her lead, they discovered it on the ground next to the shrub. Sheila wasted no time in communicating with the Marine Security Detachment at the embassy, which informed her that help was on the way.

More immediately, she turned her attention to Juan sprawled on the ground.

"Is – is he dead?" she wondered aloud.

A low moan reached her ears.

"Unfortunately, he is not," Diego replied. "I should have used a larger rock."

* *

Back in her apartment, Sheila and Diego sat in her kitchen over hot mugs of coffee.

"I should have known that you'd never arrive so late – not on your day off."

"True, but I was delayed by some mischief maker – maybe a cohort of 'Juan'. I stopped briefly at the clinic on my way here and, while I was inside, someone slashed both front tires of my car."

"Oh, no!"

"Yes – which means someone has been watching us."

"Who knows for how long?"

Diego placed an arm around her shoulder. "You are trembling," he said.

"What if – what if there are others out there?"

"My guess is that he paid some poor street kid desperate for money to delay me but, in any case, we must remain vigilant. How dared the filthy pig injure you!"

Sheila gingerly touched her bandaged jaw. "I should be counting my blessings. Thank God you came in time!"

"But you were never alone, Sheila. Our Lord never forsakes us."

"That verse of scripture came to me as he was dragging me toward the bush. He was bent on revenge – just as you warned me he might be."

"Let us forget him for now and try to relax."

"I'll try, but I can't get his laughter out of my head. He called me his *palomita.* He threatened to kill me."

He shushed her with a finger on her lips.

"I am here now. No one will harm you."

"Will you stay with me tonight?" Sheila asked.

"Nothing could tear me away."

She wanted to throw herself into his arms and remain there safely all night. *Whoa! This man is still engaged, and you're still a Foreign Service employee soon on your way to another foreign assignment, most likely never to see him again.*

She turned her face away from those limpid, dark pools – eyes that would drown her heart in its depths if she gave in to their mesmerizing force.

"I'd better get busy," she muttered. Reluctantly, she left the kitchen and headed for the linen closet. She needed to prepare the guest room bed for Diego.

* *

The good news was that after undergoing another interrogation by RSO Witt Jones, Sheila learned that Colombian authorities were holding Juan Tomás Jiménez in some secret location to circumvent the bribery and corruption that often succeeded in aiding the escape or release of many inmates. According to Jones, he wasn't privy to the tactics DAS used, but when they finished with Jiménez, "the tiger was purring like a kitten." That included confessing how he had found her. He'd simply returned to the area where he'd picked her up, assuming that she must live in or frequent that neighborhood. Among its few

Blacks, it hadn't been difficult to spot her. Surveilling the area over a few weeks yielded him the added bonus of Dr. Santos's movements. He also admitted paying a street kid to slash the doctor's tires, thus delaying the doctor's arrival at her place.

"Sheila, what's the cardinal rule about routines?"

Jones paused for dramatic effect with a raised brow, to which Sheila responded, "Never be predictable."

"But you apparently have been. How well do you know Dr. Santos?"

"We're friends."

"Yet we know that he has spent at least one night in your apartment."

"*Only* one night, and that was in the guest bedroom."

"You need not go into detail –"

"There *are* no details. I was upset; he stayed to comfort me."

"Whatever. You're adults. But the rules stand, and I trust you to abide by them. The fact that he belongs to a wealthy family may endanger him – and *you*. By the look on your face, you already knew his socio-economic status."

"Yes, but neither of us talked about it. I preferred not to dwell on the possibility of his being a magnet for kidnappers."

"Or worse. If you insist on continuing your...association with him, we'll have to brief him, and he should hire a security detail. Naturally, I trust your discretion, but you knew the risks before you got here."

"Are you saying that I shouldn't see Dr. Santos anymore?"

"That would be advisable."

The very next day, Jones sent rookie Diplomatic Security Agent Sam Sheridan to the Clínica Palermo to interview Dr. Diego Santos. The result was a report that reinforced Sheila's account of the incident and the case being closed – at least as far as the RSO was concerned. That was the good news. The bad news was that Jiménez, or rather his persona, remained with Sheila, usually in the middle of the night when certain events returned to mind.

As for the RSO's advice, she decided to again limit her contacts with Diego to the telephone – for she could no more stop associating with him than she could stop thinking of him. Diego admitted that he had selfishly risked the safety of them both and agreed that seeing her again was out of the question except, he said, in his dreams. For now, it was back to communicating solely by telephone. However, when her assignment was over and his engagement broken, they would meet again – *that* he promised. *Oh, God, speed the day!* Sheila prayed.

CHAPTER 21

The US CODEL visit to Bogotá was pressing an already busy embassy staff into overdrive. Ostensibly, the purpose of the visit was to directly assess the security situation and obtain a clear view of diplomacy in action at the post. Another purpose – unstated – was to find out if the extra 25 percent for danger pay was really necessary or if American taxpayers were being unfairly squeezed. The visit ushered in a two-day whirlwind of high-level US-Colombian Government meetings, a working dinner, press releases, increased security measures and, not surprisingly, unrealistic demands from a few delegates who complained about the restrictions. Most, however, expressed support for them. The consensus among embassy personnel was that the visit was an overall success despite the challenges that it presented. Nevertheless, they were glad to see the backs of the delegates that Friday noon.

"I don't know about you, but I could use a nice long nap," Pat announced after his return from the airport.

"Couldn't we all?" Sheila agreed with a nod, then added, "But you've been catching it from all sides, which reminds me, Mr. Sunshine. What was so urgent the other day when the

Ambassador called you to his suite – or has he sworn you to secrecy?"

Pat pulled up the nearest chair and took a deep breath. The other two officers had just left the section for lunch; he knew it was the right time to tell Sheila what he'd been avoiding so far. He cleared his throat and said, "Well, we talked mostly about you."

"Oh?" Sheila said with raised eyebrows.

"You've probably heard that the Ambassador is an agnostic. He has nothing against religion but firmly believes that it has no place in a government office. The term he actually used was *proselytizing* – that is, trying to persuade someone to convert –"

"I'm familiar with the term, Pat, but what does that have to do with me?"

"Hopefully, nothing," Pat continued, "but apparently you were seen having lunch in the embassy cafeteria with your pastor and his wife."

"And?"

"Did you invite them?"

"Yes, I did. So?"

"Well, it seems your pastor took it upon himself to invite several of our employees to his church."

"And that offended someone?"

"Not one but at least two. Sheila, he's Baptist. They're Catholic."

Sheila shrugged and commented, "Most people in this country are. I see nothing wrong with what Pastor Pittman did. In fact, I myself have been thinking of inviting you to our Sunday services."

"What!" Pat exclaimed.

"No one is obligated to accept an invitation – unless it comes from the Ambassador, of course."

"That's beside the point. The Ambassador instructed me to warn you to avoid giving even the impression of proselytizing."

"Warning taken, and don't worry, Pat. From now on, I'll do my socializing with fellow believers *outside* embassy grounds," Sheila firmly assured him.

"Now *you're* the one offended."

"No, just amazed at the Ambassador's ignorance. He obviously doesn't understand what true religion is."

"Ha!" Pat smirked in amusement. "Pretend I'm the Ambassador. Go ahead. Enlighten me."

"With all due respect, Your Excellency, James 1:27 says that pure religion is visiting widows and orphans in their trouble and keeping oneself unspotted from the world."

"That's exactly the kind of talk the Ambassador would disapprove of."

"Slightly or wholeheartedly?" Sheila asked.

"Sheila, this isn't funny."

"You don't see me laughing, do you? After all, you asked me to enlighten you."

"I didn't mean for you to *preach* to me," Pat explained, clearly annoyed. "Oh, forget it," he said in frustration, standing up and pushing the chair aside. "Just promise me that you'll watch your p's and q's from now on."

"I solemnly promise," Sheila said.

"Good," he said, sighing in relief as he turned to head for his office.

"Unless someone asks for enlightenment," she stated in a low voice.

"Sheila," Pat warned in an ominous tone.

"I have a voucher ready for your signature, Pat," Sheila parried, producing the form with a half-smile.

He almost snatched the pen from her hand, scribbled his name on the form, and quickly retreated. He was drained, both mentally and physically. Sheila knew that, but she'd still pressed her luck. Well, if she thought he was going to back down, she could think again. The Ambassador was serious. Any adverse behavior on Sheila's part was bound to reflect on him, her supervisor. He was well-known for defending his employees, but he had no intention of butting heads with the Ambassador on this or any other issue. To do so would risk his reputation and probably damage his career.

Pat himself had been a church member since the age of twelve, but he didn't go around shoving his beliefs down others' throats. His church was pretty welcoming of all people and was not known for hammering heads with mention of sin and hell's fire. It was pretty much a live-and-let-live kind of faith that he embraced. Not that Sheila was the pushy type, but the slightest impression that she was *witnessing* might rub the Ambassador the wrong way. Then, there would be too high a price to pay. Not that he believed hell actually existed.

Pat gulped down some coffee from his thermos and fortified himself with an energy bar from a stash in his desk that his wife, Liz, regularly supplied. Forcing himself to concentrate on the task at hand, he began drafting talking points for a meeting with a Colombian Government official the next week.

Sheila sat with her chin in her hand, wondering if this would be the beginning of trouble for her. She was not in the habit of proselytizing and, until today, had never been accused of doing so. On the other hand, she had never shied away from quietly sharing her faith whenever an opportunity presented itself.

As the chief executive of this dangerous post, Ambassador Váldez was carrying a heavy responsibility. She couldn't blame him for being extra-vigilant, but was his own skeptical nature pushing him toward micromanagement?

His special memo to all staff emphasized exercising extreme caution during off-duty hours to preclude any involvement with individuals who might reflect poorly on the mission and its personnel or, worse, place oneself or others in jeopardy. That made perfect sense but, of course, didn't apply to anything she was doing or failing to do. Her associations were limited to embassy personnel, those who attended the Bogotá Baptist Chapel, and once again strictly by phone with Diego. Brad Davis posed no security threat but she heartily wished he would give up trying to pursue a personal relationship with her. Lastly, there was the matter of Christy. She was a shameless flirt who knew how to get what she wanted. The whole embassy knew about Rod Radcliff's recommendation that she be immediately promoted. For what? Taking two-hour lunch breaks? Sheila instantly reined in this train of uncharitable thinking. She mustn't get caught up in the embassy's rumor mill. Gossip could be as destructive as an outright lie. She resumed working but couldn't shake off the suspicion that Christie was jealous. Ridiculous!

CHAPTER 22

Word had come down from the Drug Enforcement Administration (DEA) that, according to an informant who was undercover in the M-19, something big was going to happen – and soon. As the days went by and nothing occurred, however, the staff breathed a sigh of relief. Still, the US Mission in Colombia remained on high alert.

Patrick Carmichael, Counselor for Political Affairs, was taking his duties and the alert seriously as evidenced by the perpetual furrow on his forehead. He responded only with a sarcastic "Sure!" to Sheila's "Positive thoughts, boss."

Indeed, there was much to think positive about, Sheila concluded. Mr. Landers, the Commercial Counselor, had finally consented to an appointment with a local and well-qualified dermatologist, who recommended a biopsy. The diagnosis was second-stage melanoma, and a mole on his wrist was surgically removed soon thereafter. At his request, Mr. Landers and his wife, Portia, were quickly transferred back to the States, where he was given a position at his agency's headquarters. At the airport, Sheila had done her best to encourage them, remarking, "I'm so glad it was no worse. We'll keep you both in our prayers at the Chapel." Mrs. Landers expressed her gratitude but hovered more than ever over her husband as they waited for their departing flight number to be called.

Another thing to be thankful for was the release from captivity of James Robert Stephenson, the PENCO geologist. As expected, his company had paid the ransom to his captors, a development, Ambassador Váldez concluded, that did not bode well for any future victims held hostage by the guerillas; for he was sure that acceding to their demands would only produce more hostage taking. Sheila understood her government's policy of not negotiating with terrorists, but she was also glad for the release of the victim. Naturally, his family was overjoyed to be reunited with him.

Pat returned from the latest Country Team meeting and called Sheila and the two other Political Officers into his inner sanctum, as Sheila dubbed his office.

"To what do we owe this honor?" she asked.

He ignored the aside and immediately came to the point. "There's to be a demonstration this coming Friday, and no one knows what to expect. It's supposed to be peaceful, but some of the demonstrators most likely will be armed."

Calvin Brenner, a fifth-year employee, frowned and asked, "Does anyone know what areas we're to avoid?"

"According to Brad in Security, Séptima could be a hot spot. That's why the entire staff except the Executive Office, Communications and Security, will be sheltering in place that day. Then there's the Teatro Colón, all that area around La Candelaria. So, if any of you have plans for the symphony, cancel them. In the meantime, remember the rules – and stick to them."

The other officer, Walter Stanwyck, commented, "Frankly, all this waiting is creeping me out. We were expecting something to happen weeks ago. Are you sure somebody isn't just playing with our heads?"

"Who knows?" Pat said with a shrug. "It could be something major – or not. These guys don't send out printed invitations when they launch their events, so keep your eyes open and your heads down. And don't get careless with your radios!"

They all nodded, recalling a recent incident when one of the Junior Consular Officers left his radio in a local restaurant. Fortunately, the proprietor found it; recognized it as embassy property; and, having a cordial attitude toward the US, personally returned it to the embassy. The greenhorn got the shellacking of his life from Security. They all knew how horribly wrong that mistake could have gone. Sheila deliberately avoided Pat's pointed stare in her direction.

"Enjoy your long weekend – if you can," Pat said with a grimness that hinted they definitely wouldn't and a gesture that signaled he was finished – or so Sheila thought. As she and the other two employees started to leave, Pat motioned for her to take a seat across from his desk. He then stood up and closed the door as if to indicate that what he had to say was for her ears only.

After calling Cynthia across the hall and asking her to keep answering the section's calls a little longer, Sheila asked, "What's up, Pat?"

He frowned, reached into his desk drawer, and pulled out a sheet of paper encased in a plastic sleeve.

"This," he said, handing it over to Sheila.

She hesitated, then took the paper, and began to read. First, there was a gasp of distress, then incredulity.

"You and I? Having an affair? Caught in the act right here in your office? Pat, this is utterly insane!"

"I know it, and you know it, but somebody will need convincing that it's not true. Sheila, I've been married for almost twenty years. I've been tempted, but I've never cheated on my wife. With medication, her depression has been quite manageable for the last three years. Now this!"

"And you fear that this might bring her down again?"

"Yes, maybe even push her over the edge. Her self-esteem was once so low that she tried to –"

"You don't owe me any explanation, Pat. I understand. But who is our accuser?"

"I wish I knew. They've chosen to remain anonymous. According to the Ambassador's Office, this isn't the only copy. Several are floating around the embassy, fresh fodder for the rumor mill."

"Oh, no!" Sheila said with a groan, her head in her hands.

"Oh, yes!" Pat stated. "We could ignore the talk and wait for the rumor to die down, but you know how fast rumors can spread and the damage they can do."

"Yes, even when they're true. But we've done nothing wrong. Otherwise, why would the person who wrote this want to hide who they are?"

"Point taken. Liz is doing so well. My biggest fear is that this could set her back years."

Sheila despaired only momentarily, then, raising her head, informed Pat, "We're going to fight this. Let's start by praying."

"Sheila, what did I tell you about –?"

"It can't hurt, can it? No one, except the two of us, needs to know that we prayed."

"All right," he agreed in a dubious tone, staring at her as she bowed her head and offered a brief plea for God's wisdom and guidance, then expressing confidence that He would bring good out of a bad situation. She finished, "In the name of Jesus, we thank you. Amen."

It was over in seconds. Pat blinked in amazement, certain that he had never before heard such a simple but sincere appeal in his life. He told himself that nothing definitive would come of it, but strangely, he felt better after Sheila prayed.

"Today is Wednesday. Why don't we go home, sleep on it tonight, and keep our own counsel?"

"Good idea, Pat. Tomorrow could bring us an audience with 'His Excellency.'"

"We can always hope. Váldez just might be willing to hear us out."

"No sooner had Sheila returned to her desk and advised Cynthia, the Ambassador's Personal Assistant, to transfer their section calls back to her than Cynthia said, "Meeting over, I presume?"

"Yes," Sheila affirmed.

"Good, because you should get ready for another one. The Ambassador would like to see you and Pat right away."

When Sheila informed Pat, he donned his suit jacket; straightened his tie; and, with some trepidation, stated, "Let us proceed to the lion's den."

But with firm confidence, Sheila lifted her chin and responded, "And trust the Good Shepherd to deliver us."

An hour later, they returned to the Political Section feeling better about the situation. Pat was relieved that they had not been dismissed out of hand but respectfully listened to and assured that the allegation would be thoroughly investigated. As for Sheila, she was silently sending up a word of thanks.

Ambassador Váldez prided himself on being a pretty good judge of character. He had fielded more than one such dilemma in the past. It was obvious to him that the strong denials of these two staff members were not only sincere but also true. *Someone* wished them harm – evidently grave harm to their reputations – and he intended to get to the bottom of it. His first action was to summon Cynthia into his suite, where he dictated a memorandum to all employees, advising that any allegation of misconduct must be accompanied by the clear identification of the accuser plus the stated basis for the allegation. Unless such information was forthcoming, no action would be taken against the accused; however, the accuser would be held accountable and placed on administrative leave, initially with pay, until a thorough investigation could be conducted. Should such an allegation be proven groundless, the accuser risked at least censure or possibly a recommendation for dismissal from the Foreign Service, depending on the gravity of the allegation.

Rick Váldez had been an attorney before joining the Foreign Service Corps. Although well versed in legal jargon, he knew that he risked being not taken seriously or, worse, misunderstood. It was his intention that there be no misunderstanding. Whether true or false – and he believed the allegation to be false – he had a hunch that the rumor was fueled by malicious intent. It must stop circulating as soon as possible. Therefore, he added for good measure, "This policy is effective immediately. Should the originator not come forward within five working days from the above date, this matter will be closed."

He then instructed Cynthia, "Don't forget the full capitalization and bolding of that last sentence. And, Ms. Nelson, for emphasis, add an exclamation point."

"Yes, Mr. Ambassador," she said.

With that and a call to Regional Security Officer Witt Jones as well as all section heads in the embassy, all copies floating around the embassy were collected and replaced by the Ambassador's memo. Thus, Christy's plot was foiled since she remained anonymous and never came forward.

It was unfortunate that a more sinister plot could not have been so easily or quickly defeated.

CHAPTER 23

November 1985 was one of the bleakest months in modern Colombian history. While the vast majority of the world was shocked over the destruction caused by an earthquake in Mexico, disaster struck Colombia with two swift and deadly blows.

On Wednesday, November 6, M-19 guerillas -- some dressed as policemen, others as soldiers – gained entry to the Palace of Justice in central Bogotá. A twenty-eight-hour siege ensued. President Belisario Betancur refused to negotiate with the guerillas and demanded an unconditional surrender. Any hopes of a peaceful solution to the crisis was shattered when sporadic gunfire erupted inside the building. The Colombian military dramatically responded with heavy artillery. When it ended, fourteen judges (eleven by some press accounts), including the Chief Justice, had been executed by the guerillas before the guerillas themselves met their fate. All thirty (thirty-five by a later account) were killed. Fatalities, including other Colombian Government employees, visitors trapped inside the building, and passersby totaled approximately one hundred.

The Colombian Senate, the media, and bereaved relatives of the judges were incensed over Betancur's handling (some called it mishandling) of the crisis. Some Congressmen even demanded the President's resignation – to no avail.

Sorrow and grief had scarcely abated when exactly one week later, the Nevado del Ruiz volcano exploded in rumbling rage. Molten lava spewed up and outward, breaking and melting its gigantic ice cap. The result was a mudslide, countless tons of hot mud vaulting down the volcano's slopes to bury over twenty-four thousand inhabitants of the town of Armero under a searing blanket of death.

Colombian newspapers told and retold the stories of survivors and the dead, accompanying these dramatic accounts with graphic photographs of the horror, pictures that were to remain indelibly etched in the public's memory. Perhaps one of the most poignant dramas was that of a thirteen-year-old girl buried up to her neck in mud. She survived for about seventy hours, long enough for a rescue team to arrive, but she died of shock after finally being pulled from the mire, her leg having been caught in the grip of an already deceased aunt buried beneath her.

The nearby town of Chiva-Chiva did not altogether escape the devastation. As riverbanks overflowed, the swollen waters flooded houses, carrying many to watery graves.

The Palace of Justice takeover triggered a barrage of phone calls from anxious relatives in the States. After calling to assure her mother that she was fine, Sheila settled down to a wearying week of paperwork. The second disaster caused virtual panic, and again, telephone lines between Colombia and the United States were congested as relatives phoned to inquire if all was well with their loved ones in Colombia.

The United States was at the forefront of donations and assistance to victims of the mudslide. A "Volcano Task Force" was set up in the embassy and, among others, Sheila volunteered forty-eight hours as part of the US effort to aid the victims. She was assigned to answer telephones, type situation reports to be rushed off to the Department of State in Washington, DC, and maintain logs, listing the relief agencies arriving daily to help.

Diego called to inform Sheila that he was leaving for the region affected by the volcano. He could not say how long he would be there, but he would be in touch.

Several Colombian members of the Bogotá Baptist Chapel would be absent for the next week's Bible study in light of loved ones lost in the M-19 attack, or at Armero or Chiva-Chiva. So, the study was postponed and, in its place, a prayer vigil was held on behalf of survivors and families of the victims. It was just as well, Sheila concluded. The usual routine would benefit no one if the needs of hurting people were not addressed. What was needed at this point was encouragement, even if most could not say, "I know how you feel." Who could truly understand another's anguish unless they themselves had endured a similar experience? Hopefully, just knowing that the church cared enough to pray and help in practical ways would bring some comfort to the ones grieving.

Sheila wondered if Diego knew any of the deceased or survivors. She also worried about his safety. As a doctor, exposure to pain and suffering would be nothing new to him. Still, he was only human; and the scale of the tragedy might take a heavy emotional, if not physical, toll on him. She was convinced that her episode with "Juan" was an unfortunate *fluke*, but she was very much afraid that Diego, being the son of a wealthy businessman, was at true risk of being gravely harmed. Why had neither of them considered that before? Had love blinded them to the dangers or had they escaped harm by the mercy of God? Perhaps it was a good thing that he was away right now; perhaps it was even more critical that they maintain physical distance between each other. Before going to bed that night, she knelt to pray for him and the many families affected. She tried to calm her troubled thoughts by remembering Philippians 4:6. "Be anxious for nothing." No, she must not worry. Worrying indicated a lack of faith. The antidote to worry was in the same passage, which continued, "But in everything by prayer and supplication and thanksgiving, let your requests be made known to God."

Not worrying was easier said than done. She tried to pray, even repeating the Lord's Prayer, but the words sounded hollow and rehearsed. Recalling news photos, especially those taken at Armero, triggered a restlessness that had her tossing and turning half the night. With Diego's face haunting her dreams, she awakened exhausted and in dread of another workday. Nevertheless, she pushed herself to get ready and was waiting in the apartment lobby when the embassy van arrived to pick her up. This time, the guard motioned away the little group of street kids even as she slipped a couple of coins into an outstretched palm. Then, she sprinted toward the armored van and was quickly hustled inside by an Uzi-armed guard, who leaped into the chase car.

Once safely inside the embassy building, Sheila sent up a silent petition for calmness and proceeded to the office. The routine of opening safes, file cabinets and a vault before brewing a pot of coffee (which some office managers refused to do) might as well have been done by a robot. She was simply going through the motions without engaging her mind. Finally, at midmorning, she forced herself to focus on getting a diplomatic note typed with the usual closing phrase about mutual interests. Then, she began finalizing three pages of talking points for Calvin Brenner. Just as she finished proofreading the latter document, the Marine Security Guard in the lobby called to inform her that an envelope had just been dropped off by courier for her. Asking Cynthia to cover the section's incoming calls for a few minutes, she rushed downstairs, her heart racing. She viewed the return address and wept for joy. The official stationery of Doctors Without Borders indicated that the sender was Diego. Resisting the urge to open the envelope immediately, she retreated to the restroom to wash her face and lightly reapply her makeup. She did not trust her own emotions at the moment and decided to delay reading the letter until she was in her apartment. First, she must get through the day with some semblance of maturity – for her bout of nerves was totally out of character for the savvy and level-headed woman she tried to be.

The embassy remained on high alert. Diplomatic Security Agents Jones and Davis regularly met with their Colombian contacts, who advised that the death of those M-19 guerillas had increased, not lessened, the threat to American lives. The FARC was equally determined to accelerate its campaign against the US and Colombian Governments.

The timing of the letter's delivery followed several days after the two big headlines. It was also the same day that a handheld rocket, positioned from the rear passenger window of a sedan, was launched into the embassy's roof. The rocket's nose pierced the ceiling of the Communications Section. No one was injured, but the staff of that section was traumatized.

There was immense relief when the no-parking zones around the embassy's chancery were extended, and the van schedules and routes were further randomized.

Despite the attack that day, nothing could dampen Sheila's excitement in anticipation of getting to her apartment, where she could read Diego's letter in total privacy. As soon as she got home that evening, Sheila put on a kettle of water to boil for tea, then kicked off her shoes and flopped down onto the sofa, impatient and giddy all at once. Opening the envelope with fumbling fingers, she began to read,

My dear Sheila,

Getting mail into and out of this area is difficult, so I am sending this letter to you by courier in Manizales. Hopefully, you will receive it quickly. May it find you well in every way.

I am here in Armero as a member of a volunteer medical team. These past few days have been grueling. The awesome force of nature cannot but humble any man, and I am no exception. It brings the realization of how brief this life is. The Chapel should do a study of Job ("Man born of woman is of few days and full of trouble"), no? I have never before seen such devastation. I cannot tell you how difficult it has been to contain my sorrow in the face of such tragedy for thousands. Most of the survivors were the poorest inhabitants of Armero, living on higher ground at the edge of the city. Most have minimal education and only manual skills to offer any employer.

The Red Cross is still in the area, distributing food and clothing to the people; we of the medical team have more-than-adequate supplies. Catholic Relief Services has also been very generous, among many others.

There is word that a new Armero will be built nearby to replace the one that was destroyed, but the survivors would prefer a location far away from this area where they would not have to look down on their old city, now completely buried. It is a bleak prospect, but these people have no choice. They must be housed somewhere and carry on with their lives no matter what memories such a view may evoke. Tents have been erected temporarily.

Every morning, I get up to watch the sunrise. I marvel at how such beauty can persist in the face of destruction, yet it does. The Nevado del Ruiz is softly rumbling, and even it, with its ugly heart of death, is still beautiful to gaze upon.

Please forgive the lack of cheer in this letter. You are the one person I can share this with, except perhaps my sister, Concepción. Even so, one cannot be too graphic in describing the scene here; hers is quite a sensitive nature. She is sixteen years younger than Your Servant and aspires to be a physician also someday despite our father's opposition. (He believes that women of a certain class should not work.)

God willing, I shall return to Bogotá before the end of this month. I will call you as soon as I arrive.

Until then,

Diego

Sheila sighed in frustration. There was nothing, not a modicum of romance in this letter. Well, what had she hoped for? That he would once again bare his soul to her? Their relationship remained in limbo as long as he was engaged to be married. The most that either of them could hope for in the short term was what they were restricted to right now – this letter and phone calls when he returned. And in the long term? She mustn't think too far ahead. Dejectedly, she folded the letter, placed it back in its envelope, and decided to write to her mother and Kevin.

146

CHAPTER 24

Christy Welles seethed with jealousy, reliving the night that she had seen Diego and Sheila at Tramonti's. From a shadowed nook where she and Rod had been sequestered, she'd observed the look of pure adoration on the doctor's face. As if that weren't enough, one of the young Marines let slip that his duty had been anything but ordinary recently when he'd had to send security to Sheila's aid. Apparently, an irate taxi driver had crossed the line (probably over an exorbitant fare that she refused to pay), but upon arrival at the scene, who had already rescued the little Black damsel in distress and clobbered the guy? None other than the handsome Dr. Santos!

Although her scheme to smear Sheila and, consequently, Pat, had failed, she still could not get over her temporary failure to snare the doctor. But how was she to do that with Rod constantly breathing down her neck? He had begun slipping little handwritten messages under her desk blotter every morning and calling her apartment every evening, barely harnessing a passion that defied all logic. Attempting to apply a cold dash of reality to his heated declarations of love, Christy warned him that if they weren't careful, they would be found out. But he recklessly cried, "I don't care! I'm crazy about you!" He was voicing exactly how she felt about Diego Santos – well, not exactly. She wasn't really in love with him, but Christie had just found out that he was financially flush. Getting rid of Rod was key. Wearing disposable gloves, Christy addressed a letter to Rod's wife in the States (having secured the address from Rod's own office file document indicating "next of kin"). Crafted to be thought- and perhaps anger-provoking, it posed the question, "Do you trust your husband completely?" Then, coming to the point, it stated, "If you do, you're naïve." The note ended with a warning that if she wanted to save her marriage, she'd better get smart – and fast.

The note to Rod Radcliff's wife brought swift results. Amanda Radcliff wasted no time in contacting her husband by phone. She demanded to know if he was cheating on her. Totally dumbfounded for a split second, Radcliff indignantly took issue with the accusation, exclaiming, "Of course not! Wherever did you get that idea?" She responded that she had her sources, and if he hadn't cheated, it probably wasn't for lack of trying. To this, he had no comment, which convinced her that she was right. Slamming down the receiver of the phone, she called the Ambassador himself next. She informed him of the anonymous letter and requested that he consider curtailing her husband's assignment. When he stated that he did not place much confidence in anonymous notes and suggested that she try to work out her differences with her husband, she informed him that that was exactly what she intended to do, but in the States – not long distance. If he wasn't willing to help her, she would find someone who was, she angrily declared.

Váldez had no desire to play the role of a marriage counselor. He was a diplomat and, as such, he had been as tactful as he knew how to be. Still, he did not require much persuading. Deputy Chief of Mission Charlemagne was still deeply concerned over the Consular Section's backlog. Adding another employee would not solve the problem. Transferring Radcliff to Washington, DC, would. The backlog was a valid issue, one that easily overrode any marital issues as far as he was concerned. Váldez knew of a certain retired female diplomat who would fill the vacancy admirably until a replacement for Radcliff could be assigned. And so, on official grounds of "compassion," the Consular Chief was being granted an early "home leave." During that gap, he could bid on his next (and probably final) assignment.

Desperate to maintain his contact with Christy, Radcliff promised her that he would find a way for them to be together. In the meantime, the date of his departure was approaching fast and, once again, he reserved the cottage for the weekend. His amorous scheme, however, stalled when not just another migraine but heavy menstrual cramping had Christy confined to bed. Then, because of more terrorist threats, the staff had to shelter in place again, evaporating his hopes of being with Christy before he had to board the plane for DC and Amanda awaiting him.

* *

After Radcliff's departure, Christy's behavior changed drastically. Having received official word that her promotion had been approved, she saw no reason not to appease the interim supervisor. She might have to go back to her usual strategy at the next assignment but for the time being, she had only one goal in mind: a night – or two - with Diego Santos. No man had ever rejected her. She couldn't remotely imagine *his* doing so. He certainly wouldn't favor *Sheila* over her. At the time, divorce was illegal in Colombia, but marriage was not her goal. She craved the conquest of that delectable beefcake for her own private pleasure with no entanglements. One night with her, and he'd be begging for more.

After managing to get an appointment, Christy dressed in a skimpy outfit that emphasized her curvaceous figure. At the clinic, she was placed in an examining room and was attended, not by Dr. Santos but by a colleague of his, a Dr. Suárez, who was young but woefully lacking in looks. She left, only slightly deflated by this latest setback. When her repeated efforts to see him met with his "unavailability," however, she was stunned. Her vanity would not allow her to even imagine that she was other than irresistible except, of course, to those men with *closeted* tendencies. In that case, she'd be wasting her time anyway. She supposed that Diego Santos, as manly as he appeared, might not be what he seemed. Well, one way or another she was going to find out.

CHAPTER 25

Brad Davis knew that Sheila's tour of duty in Bogotá would end soon. Christmas would arrive in only a week's time, then spring would be right around the corner and she'd be departing for home leave and training for her next assignment. If he was going to make any headway with her, now was the time. But, ever since Santos had rescued her from that taxi driver, he had been striking out with her – well, if he were honest, it was long before that but that little adventure seemed to seal the deal for her—or had it? He'd been casing her movements after work, so he knew that she wasn't dating the doctor any more. Then, he discovered from a source at the Clínica Palermo that Santos was still in Armero volunteering his medical services there. That should have provided him, Brad, a window to nab her, but she kept making excuses not to go out with him. Could it be that despite the doctor's absence, she had actually *fallen* for him? Brad had been instantly attracted to her, and his ego would not let him give up without a fight.

In his encounters with women, his creed had always been "out of sight, out of mind" as he quickly moved on to the next conquest. This, however, was different. Like a bolt out of the blue, his need for her had evolved into something deeper than passion. He knew that he had finally found the ideal woman, and he intended to marry her. It did not occur to him that his conceit and arrogance in presuming that he could win her were flaws of character that would push her away, not attract her.

Once the latest shelter-in-place order was lifted, he wasted no time. Stopping by her desk the very next day, he poured on the charm again. Weary of being polite, Sheila finally told him, "Brad, you're trying too hard. You and I both know it won't work."

"You slay me, baby!" he exclaimed with a dramatic palm-over-heart motion. "You've never really given me a chance."

"Well, I guess it hardly matters now," Sheila commented. "I'll soon be gone."

"Gone, but not forgotten."

"I believe that line is popular at funerals," she said.

"Once you leave, this place will feel like a tomb," Brad remarked, leaning closer to gauge her reaction.

"You're good!" Sheila exclaimed, laughing so loudly that it punctured his pride.

"Sheila, I'm serious," he said, his mood suddenly sober and oddly appealing.

"I apologize, Brad. That was rude of me."

"And you're willing to make it up to me at dinner tonight?"

"Not dinner. I'm already culling my possessions for the sale on Saturday. Spring will be here before we know it, and I want to have everything ready and organized when the packers arrive."

"That's months away."

"Not the sale. That's only two days away."

"And you can't spare an hour to have a drink after work?"

"I think you know that I'm a teetotaler except for the occasional glass of wine."

"Then have your wine or a soda – on me." When she hesitated, he said, "I promise not to keep you out too late."

"All right, Brad."

"See you at seven."

And with that, Brad Davis returned to the Security Office, eager for the end of the workday when he could be with the woman he wanted so desperately. Then, his thoughts turned to Diego Santos. His jaw tightened. He could almost hear his mother's voice, "Be angry and do not sin." He was well acquainted with Psalm 4:4. Her reprimands had always been gentle, while his father's words were harsh and condemning, "And be sure your sin will find you out." How could he ever forget Numbers 32:23? His father made him quote it aloud each time he found fault with Brad – which was often. For a moment, he felt regret about how disappointed his parents, knowing him as they did, must be in him – but he quickly shoved their Biblical wisdom aside. He had had his fill of all that and was living life on his own terms. Yet, he couldn't deny, even to himself, that he was angry, and he was proud, but he had a right to be.

As the number two man in Security, he was privy to every reported incident. Perhaps no one could have anticipated or averted what happened to Sheila in that dark field, but had Sheila chosen to confide in him instead of Santos, he might have – no, *would have* been the one to rescue her when "Juan" showed up, bent on revenge. Instead, he concluded bitterly, it was Santos who had snatched that chance away from him. Brad clenched and unclenched his fists, taking long, deep breaths.

He didn't understand the hold the woman had on him. He only knew that it was real – and strange. Easy, naïve, vulnerable, weak – those were the women he'd always been attracted to. Color, class, race? He was an equal-opportunity kind of guy as long as he got what he wanted. Sheila didn't fit the former caveats. Was that why he found her so irresistible? But, there was one kind of woman he despised – the vixen. Like a spider, she wove her web of seduction to snare the fly. He thought of Christy. Initially, he found her physically alluring, but he was quickly repelled as he observed her prowess in action. Poor Radcliff! She was not the type to yield to another's power, and neither was Brad. In that regard, they were alike. From some subtle remark she'd once made, the fact that he was Black was a strike against him. His second position in the RSO also failed to score points with her. It was clear that she preferred men with power, money or both. Well, once he'd met Sheila, he hadn't spared Christy a second glance.

Brad was in a good mood for the rest of the day. Santos was still in Armero. Sheila was here in Bogotá, and so was he. This was the night! By the time he left the office, he was practically rubbing his hands with glee.

****

Like all direct-hire US citizen employees, Brad and Sheila arrived at work in an armor-plated van and were delivered back to their respective apartments the same way. She freshened up and dressed in a casual white blouse and navy A-line skirt; Brad took extra care with his appearance after a long hot shower, splashing on a lemon-scented cologne. By the time he arrived at seven p.m. to pick up Sheila, he felt almost light-headed at the prospect of the evening ahead. She dashed out of the lobby, quickly entered his red BMW, and off they went to a small café in the neighborhood where he lived.

"Isn't this Santa Barbara?" Sheila asked.

"It is," Brad replied. "This place serves the best *empanadas*. Is there a problem?"

"No, it's just that it's farther than I thought we'd be. El Chico Grande has good cafés too."

"Yes, but that's *your* neighborhood. I'm more familiar with this area."

She didn't argue the point but smiled rather stiffly, wondering if this was to be just for drinks, as he'd said.

They talked casually until her soda and his beer arrived, then bit into fresh, warm *empanadas* served on the side. The flaky thin pockets, filled with tender beef, were cooked to perfection.

"Delicious!" she remarked.

"I told you, didn't I?"

They finished the *empanadas* before he turned the conversation to her next assignment.

"I suppose there's a high probability that you'll get your top choice."

"Maybe, maybe not. If I get Mexico City or La Paz, I won't need the language training but I'll still have to review the *Background Notes*."

"La Paz. Now why would you include that? Certainly, you're aware of the extremely high altitude".

"Of course, I am. But my mother wants me closer to the States."

"What are your other preferences?"

"Paris, Seoul, Tokyo, and Zagreb."

"I hope you get Paris."

"Thanks. The idea of total immersion language and cultural training isn't all that appealing. Even French could pose a big challenge. I haven't spoken it since I was in high school – and that was a very long time ago."

"Don't give me that! What are you – twenty-five, twenty-six?"

"I just turned twenty-nine, and don't forget that I'm the mother of a rambunctious little boy."

"But not too rambunctious for his beautiful mother to handle," he commented in a suave tone, which Sheila deliberately ignored.

When he noticed her checking the time on her watch, he said, "I promised not to keep you out too late, so let's get out of here."

She nodded, relieved when he paid the bill and escorted her to his car.

As they headed back to her apartment building, he reminisced about his tour of duty in France.

"When were you there?" Sheila asked.

"Five years ago. The food here is good, but when you've had the best –" he shrugged, letting the sentence trail off.

To Sheila's amazement, he pulled into an area away from the building's well-lit entrance. "Why are we stopping here?" she asked.

"Why do you ask?" Brad countered.

"I'm just curious. It's dark over here."

"I wanted us to have some privacy before you go in. There's something important I need to say."'

"All right, Brad. What is it?"

"I think you know how I feel about you, Sheila."

"You mean how you feel about women in general."

"OK, that's fair. I'm no monk. I've had my share of women, but this is not the same. With you, it's different. Sheila, baby, I'm in love with you. Marry me!"

"Marry you?" Sheila said in a shocked tone. "Brad, I hardly know you."

"How well did you get to know Diego Santos during the month I was gone?"

"Brad, that's unfair. We attended the same Wednesday-night Bible studies."

"What about the flowers? Does the doctor always send flowers to every lady he studies with?"

Sheila giggled. "That would certainly put a dent in his wallet. There are at least a dozen women in the group, including seven who are married. Their husbands might have something to say about that."

"What about the rescue from that scumbag 'Juan'?"

"The doctor was coming there anyway to pick me up for the Bible study."

"He sounds too good to be true," Brad said with an ironic twist to his mouth, adding, "So he means nothing to you?"

"Brad, this line of questioning is uncalled for. Dr. Santos is engaged."

"Does that mean you're willing to give me a chance? Oh, I'm not talking about eloping. We could keep in touch. I want to meet your family, prove that I can be a good husband to you and a good dad to your son –"

Sheila was shaking her head. "I'm sorry Brad, but I don't feel the same about you."

"Come on, Sheila, level with me. There's some reason I can't make any headway with you. I saw that bleeding-heart act on the balcony at your party – or was it real?"

"Bleeding heart? Oh, that! That was just for Christy's benefit. You know what a flirt she is."

"OK. Don't give me your answer tonight, but know this: I won't let Santos or anybody else come between us. I'm ready to take our relationship to the next level."

"We don't have a relationship. You're a colleague and, I hope, a friend. I wouldn't hurt you for the world, but can't you see? We have nothing in common."

"Have you looked in a mirror lately?"

"I mean common interests and shared values. I wouldn't consider marrying someone who doesn't share my faith."

"Now you're beginning to sound like a religious nut. 'Do not be unequally yoked together with unbelievers.' Don't look so surprised. I know the lingo. After all, I was a PK."

"A preacher's kid? Brad, what happened?"

"What *didn't* happen?" he said, his voice tinged with bitterness. Then, directing a look at her that hinted at rising anger, he asked, "What could you and Santos possibly have in common?"'

When Sheila didn't reply, he challenged, "Come on, tell me!"

"What is this – an interrogation?" she asked.

"No. Just try to see my side of it. I go out of town on business for a month, and you and Santos become the hottest news since the bomb exploded. I'm probably the butt of every joke at the embassy."

"Brad, nobody's laughing at you. Why would they?"

"I've never hidden my feelings for you."

"Maybe you should have. I'm sorry, but like I told you, I don't feel the same."

"You would if Santos weren't in the picture," he flung at her. She started to protest, but he cut her off. "Have you slept with him? Is that it?"

"I told you before. The man is engaged."

"Do I look like a fool?"

"Are you judging him by your own standards?"

"He's a man, isn't he? Or is he?"

"Brad, you haven't been listening to me."

"I heard you loud and clear. I'm not going to beat my fists into the pillow all night if you admit you slept with him. We can put it all behind us. Baby, I want you, not just for a night but for keeps. Hey, we're both Black. It's natural that we should be together. Give us a chance!"

His voice throbbed with urgency. He had said he loved her, but she doubted if he knew the meaning of the word – the long-term commitment and sacrifice required. It was useless to argue with him.

"It's getting late, and I still have things to do tonight," she said.

"Oh, yes. The culling! Excuse me if I prefer *cuddling*!" he scoffed. He was shaking his head as if in total denial. "I can't believe this is happening. Black women in the States are ready to slit our throats for looking at White women, always complaining that there aren't enough brothers to go around. But Santos enters the picture and suddenly, I'm toast."

Sheila was losing patience now and decided to get to the crux of the matter. "Brad, you've crossed the color line, so you have no right to lecture me."

"All right, I've had White women, but they didn't mean a thing to me. Given a choice –"

"You had a choice. What you're saying is that I don't deserve the same thing. You're a hypocrite, Brad."

"No. You're the hypocrite. Lying about what's going on between you and Santos. He spent a night in your apartment. Don't tell me the two of you were reciting poetry!"

"Please, listen to me!"

"I've heard all I need to hear. There's a name for sisters like you!" Brad hissed, his eyes burning with something akin to hatred.

"I'm going in now, Brad," Sheila said with a sigh of frustration. She picked up her purse from the floor of the car.

"No, you're not."

The ugliness in his voice made her glance up. The expression on his face was all too revealing. His ego had taken a severe beating. Instinctively, she realized the vulnerability of her own situation and acted accordingly but not quickly enough. Her door was unlocked, her hand on the handle, when she was savagely jerked back against him. She shivered in revulsion, then struggled to break free.

"Let … me go! Let me go!" she demanded, her breath coming in ragged gasps, her words unheeded.

"Shut up!" he snapped, shaking her as if she were no more than a rag doll. "You've sold out, you –"

The insult was suspended as a gust of cold air rushed in upon them when the door on her side was flung open. Briefly caught off guard, Brad loosened his hold. Sheila threw herself out of the car and up against the hard wall of a man's chest.

"Are you alright?" he asked.

She almost collapsed in relief. It was Diego. Before she could answer, however, Brad had gotten out of his car and was advancing upon them with clenched teeth and murderous eyes.

"Santos," he snarled, "you're a dead man!"

"Am I?" Diego quietly responded, leveling the barrel of a revolver toward his heart.

Brad halted and took a step forward. "You're bluffing," he taunted.

"Try me," came the challenge.

Brad backed off, got back into his car and, on screeching tires, sped away as if being chased by demons.

Sheila stood trembling within the circle of Diego's arms.

"It is over now, *pequeña*, all over," he consoled in a low voice.

She understood the endearment. He had called her *little one*, and it jolted her back to a moment of clarity. Diego was here – really here. She could hardly take it in.

"Is it?" she asked. "Then why are you shaking as much as I am?"

"It is the revolver," he admitted.

"You *were* bluffing," she whispered.

"Yes."

"What if he hadn't believed you? Would you have fired at his feet?"

"No, I could not have."

She moved back to stare up into his face with incredulous eyes.

He nodded almost imperceptibly. "You understand. The gun is not loaded."

He was quite solicitous, holding her until she calmed down and her mind was uncluttered enough to ask how he came to be there at precisely the moment she needed him.

"I called to let you know that I was back, but after repeated calls and no answer, I decided to come. I began to sense that something was wrong," he explained.

"Didn't it occur to you that I might have gone out for the evening?" Sheila asked.

"I suppose not. You have never *not* answered before."

Feeling still somewhat unnerved, she asked if he would see her up to her apartment.

"Gladly," he replied. "I wish to know what happened between you and Davis."

Inside the apartment, Diego built a fire and extended his hands toward the flames in the fireplace. As she provided him the details surrounding Brad's explosive behavior, his eyes narrowed.

"Did he hurt you?" he asked.

"Only with his words. Let's forget him. He's probably on the way to licking his wounds with some other woman by now."

"Licking his wounds?" Diego queried with a puzzled look.

Sheila explained, "It's slang for trying to salvage his pride."

Struggling to fill the awkward silence hanging heavily between them now, she asked if he made a habit of carrying a gun.

"Not at all. My father gave it to me years ago and insisted I keep it in the glove compartment in case I became the target of robbers – or worse. I confess. I forgot to purchase ammunition for it."

"Yet you dared to confront Brad Davis with it."

"I had to. In a physical fight, I would have been no match for him. I had to outwit him."

"And you did. Once again, I'm in your debt."

"As I am in yours," he responded, followed by a deep chest cough. Her raised eyebrows prompted him to add, "If you have some soup for a starving man."

"And if I'm not mistaken, one who's also sick," she said, retreating to the kitchen to prepare canned soup and a pot of coffee, which brought back bittersweet memories. When she returned to the living room with the tray, however, it was obvious that the hunger in his eyes had nothing to do with needs of the stomach. She said the first thing that popped into her head and could have kicked herself for veering into forbidden territory.

"Nothing has been resolved between you and your father, I take it?"

"I have not spoken to him since I left. I returned only this afternoon. I know that his deepest dread is my bringing scandal upon our family or hers. I am asking that you keep trusting me. When … when do you leave?"

"March."

"And your next assignment is –?"

"I don't know yet. I'll probably be informed in January. In the meantime, we are still restricted to telephone contact."

He consumed the soup, emptied his mug, and set the tray on the coffee table.

"Christmas is almost here," he said, a note of sadness in his voice. "I wish we could spend it together."

"That would be nice, but –"

"We cannot," he finished her sentence and began coughing again. "How I managed to convince Davis of my – toughness, I will never know."

"Thank you, Diego."

"No, thank *you* for – being patient with me, for –" another cough erupted. He was thinner, his face had stubble, his eyes looked sunken and glassy, and there was about his entire frame a weariness that overshadowed his attempts to suppress his spasmodic coughing. The only thing that appeared to be unchanged was the softly curling raven-black hair on his head, which needed trimming. But that was the least of Sheila's concerns at the moment.

"I suggest you go home and get some rest. You sound terrible," she said.

"And I probably look terrible," he remarked. "But I am not going home – at least not yet. For now, I … I am renting… a room in the house of my colleague, Dr. Lorenzo Suárez. You have… my number at the clinic. You can reach me there or leave… a message."

He gave her one lingering gaze as if committing the sight of her to memory. "I suppose the… Bible studies at the Chapel have been… suspended indefinitely?"

"Yes. I miss them."

"As do I," he said with another eloquent look hinting that she too was missed, then added, "we will continue to speak by telephone."

"As soon as you're better. I'll be praying for you."

"Then I cannot ask for more –"

"Or offer more," Sheila said.

"Or offer more," he softly repeated, reaching for her hands and pressing each one to his lips before intoning, "Que Dios te bendiga." At the door, he turned and said, "Do not forget to wash your hands."

Sheila looked down, searching for some visible matter on them. She looked up, frowning.

"The germs – from my lips. I do not wish you to be infected with whatever I have," he said with a wistful smile. Then, he was gone.

She listened to the whir of the elevator as he descended to the lobby, left the building and walked to his Mustang. Rushing to the balcony, she watched him get in and drive away, tears filling her eyes.

"May God bless you too, darling," she whispered before reluctantly going to the kitchen sink to wash her hands.

"May God bless you too, darling," she whispered before reluctantly going to the kitchen sink to wash her hands.

CHAPTER 26

As Diego drove away, another spasm of coughing hit him. He had to pull over onto the shoulder of a side street to keep the car stable. Inhaling and exhaling deeply, he sat for several minutes, thinking about what had just happened. He had left Sheila when he wanted so much to stay. Yet, he knew that prolonging his time with her would have ended in his yielding to the temptation of taking her in his arms and kissing not only her hands but her lips. It was better that he'd left when he did, and not only because of the germs he would spread from his mouth to hers. She had been through enough, and he did not need to add to her stress. When all was said and done, one fact remained: His engagement to Rosa Galán hung between them like a sword of judgment, ready to slash any hopes of a future together for them.

He lay his aching head upon the steering wheel and groaned aloud. In a few months, she would be leaving and, already, he was feeling the void that distance would impose on him. Would she feel the same? Would he be able to free himself from his present dilemma before she left? He had to recover his strength first. He pulled back onto the street, soon arriving at the colonial house where friend and colleague Lorenzo

Suárez lived. Twilight was giving way to darkness, and as he rang the doorbell under the lit archway, he braced himself for the rebuke that he knew was coming.

Alicia – the chubby, grey-haired little housekeeper – cautiously peered through the peephole, then opened the door wide, frowning.

"*Don* Diego, hurry!" she exclaimed, motioning him inside. "The good doctor has been anxiously awaiting your return. You know that he was quite against your going out this evening."

"I know, I know, Alicia, but it was necessary," Diego explained.

"Was it?" a steel-edged voice boomed from the vestibule. There stood Lorenzo – young, tall, and fit in a plush cream bathrobe, arms crossed and eyes narrowed.

Diego expected a scolding but, instead, saw a flicker of compassion.

"I was worried, old man," Lorenzo informed him.

"I am sorry about that, Lorenzo, but I had to go. As I suspected, she needed my help."

"And you need ours," Lorenzo stated, then addressed the housekeeper, "Prepare the bath, Alicia."

After a warm bath, Diego was hustled into a freshly turned-down bed. Lorenzo was standing at the foot of the bed. He gestured to Alicia. "Bring the tray."

"Do not bother. I have eaten already," Diego informed them.

"It is only *caldo*," Lorenzo said.

"Breakfast broth? Then I will have it in the morning."

"As you wish," Lorenzo responded with a shrug.

Diego rubbed his temples and slumped back against a mound of pillows.

"Bring my medical bag, Alicia," Lorenzo instructed.

Lorenzo took Diego's temperature and blood pressure; listened to his heart and lungs; and examined his tongue, eyes, ears, and fingernails. Then, putting the instruments aside, he announced, "You have a low-grade fever. I believe the phlegm in your lungs began with an ear infection. A five-day course of antibiotics should clear it up. But first things first."

Turning to the housekeeper, he directed, "Alicia, prepare the lemon-honey tea, then see to the unpacking."

"I can unpack my bags myself," Diego said.

Lorenzo frowned. "This is no time to play Mr. Self-Sufficient. Quickly, Alicia!"

"She need not hurry, Lorenzo. You behave as if I am at death's door."

"You soon may be if you do not follow orders."

"Orders," Diego repeated with a weak grin that became a grimace as the coughing resumed.

He slept soundly that night and rested well the next day. The following day after that, he awakened early, intent on taking a brief shower and a walk around the neighborhood. However, as he raised himself up on one elbow, the faithful housekeeper was at his bedside to plump up the pillows behind his head.

"¡*Pobrecito!*" She consoled, gently pushing him onto his back. Poor little one? He did not need her pity. He needed fresh air and exercise.

He politely asked her to pardon him, but the words were muffled as she wiped his mouth and entire face with a warm washcloth and then began applying lotion.

"Alicia, please," he implored, pushing her hand away.

"What a fine head of hair you have, *Don* Diego," she said, bringing forth a soft-bristled brush.

"Alicia!" he exclaimed.

Her hand halted in mid-air. She stepped back and, with clasped hands, respectfully addressed him, "It is a privilege to serve you *Don* Diego."

"Thank you, Alicia, but at the moment, I do not require your services. Now, will you excuse me?"

"Please to let me know when you are ready for the *caldo, Don* Diego," she said, turning to leave the bedroom.

Diego proceeded to the guest bathroom. By the time he had showered, shaved and dressed, Lorenzo had already left for the clinic. There was a note from him on the kitchen table, advising that he would be home at about six. In the meantime, Diego was to make himself comfortable, go at a slow pace today, and make Alicia feel useful. "She likes to keep busy."

Obviously, Diego dryly concluded.

By the time Lorenzo got home, it was 7:00 pm, and Diego was seated on a bench in the small rear garden. He was deep in thought. Lorenzo's hand on his shoulder startled him.

"Hiding from Alicia?" he teased.

"No, no. In fact, she and I became better acquainted today. Lorenzo, she was widowed as a young woman, lost her husband

and children in a plane crash, and has no near kin. No wonder she fusses about so much. She is a lonely soul."

"I am well aware of the circumstances of Alicia's life. After all, she has been in my employ the last three years. But, *amigo*, do not tell me that you are out here brooding over the misfortunes of an elderly widow whom you hardly know." When Diego remained silent, Lorenzo remarked, "As soon as we got here from the airport two days ago, you began calling… her, I presume."

"Yes," Diego admitted, "but she never answered, so I had to know if she was safe."

"As ill as you were, you rushed out of here with no regard for your own condition. This American – you fancy yourself in love with her?"

"You sound like my father."

"Then it is true? You are willing to give up everything for this woman?"

"Her name is Sheila."

"But she is *morena*?

"Yes, she is dark."

"Does Rosa know of the affair?"

Diego rose to his feet and, there, in the lamplight of the garden, squarely faced his friend. "There has been no affair, but Sheila knows that I love her."

"But for this … love, you must not do anything foolish, Diego."

"Foolish? No, Lorenzo. Her assignment ends next Spring. For now, we are keeping our distance."

"For now? Are you saying that you intend to keep pursuing this woman … this Sheila?" Lorenzo asked, his voice rising an octave.

"With everything in me," Diego fervently declared. Once I break my engagement to Rosa, I will ask Sheila to marry me."

Lorenzo was shaking his head in amazement. How could Diego forfeit a fiancée as pretty as her name? He himself had been legally separated from his wife for the last year, so he knew that making marriage a success was hard work. But, in Diego's case, there was the Galán fortune to sweeten the bargain. Had his friend lost all common sense?

As these thoughts raced through his head, Alicia entered the garden.

"*Don* Diego, you have a visitor," she announced.

Lorenzo took the card from her outstretched hand, read it, and passed it along to his friend.

"Wait, Diego," he said, placing a detaining hand on his arm. "You are in no condition to deal with your father tonight. Let me handle this."

Without waiting for Diego's response, he ordered Alicia to bring the lemon and honey tea for Dr. Santos before returning to the house to greet Fabio Santos. Ten minutes later, he was back.

"So soon?" Diego queried. "Was he insistent? What did you tell him?"

Lorenzo put up a hand. "Patience, Diego. One thing at a time. Firstly, he played the *hidalgo* to the hilt, greeting me with a bow and handshake. Then he asked about my health and my wife, knowing full well that we are no longer together. Secondly, he said he hoped all was well at the Clínica Palermo, and he supposed you are on duty again."

"How did he know of my return? Surely, you did not phone him."

"Absolutely not. One of his contacts at the airport must have done so. Thirdly, he said he had reliable information that you are living here."

"You digress, Lorenzo."

"Sorry. To get to the point —"

"Please!" Diego begged.

"I told him that you are here but that you are not yet well enough to resume your duties or even to receive visitors. At this, he expressed concern and inquired as to your specific ailment." Lorenzo paused deliberately to gauge his friend's mood.

"And?" Diego prodded.

"I told him that an infection in the lungs is not to be taken lightly. Therefore, regretfully, I could not permit my patient to be disturbed, but I would gladly relay a message on *His Grace's* behalf. Of course, I did not explain that your greater ailment is lovesickness," Lorenzo said with a grin.

Diego could not help but smile. "Lorenzo, I thank you. Now tell me. Did he have a message for me?"

"Indeed, he did. Rosa is quite upset. I believe the word he used was *hysterical*. A private detective informed her father of your betrayal with the American. Rosa is threatening to break the engagement and to ruin you publicly unless you renounce the affair and beg her forgiveness."

Diego's tone was grim. "So, like you, she believes there was an affair. The hysteria is probably an act. She has never given me any indication that she cares for anything other than the social status I can bring to her family. As for the threat, I will lose no sleep over it."

"At least, it is only a threat, *amigo*. Believe me, the affair will become a distant memory once you reconcile with her. You are – how do the *gringos* say? – a good catch."

"I repeat: there was no affair! Furthermore, I have no intention of reconciling with Rosa. Sheila is the only woman I want."

Lorenzo stared at him. "What are you going to do?"

Diego smiled and said, "I am going to plan a wedding, Lorenzo. The sooner the better."

Lorenzo touched Diego's forehead with the back of one hand.

"The fever is gone, but so is the ability to reason," he teased.

"I assure you, *amigo*, that my ability to reason is better than ever," Diego said, a new light of optimism shining in his eyes.

CHAPTER 27

Word of Brad Davis's death spread throughout the embassy like a brush fire. He had rounded a mountain bend much too fast, tumbled over a cliff, and crashed to the valley floor.

Although relieved that she never again would have to face his terrifying anger, Sheila deeply regretted the argument that had preceded his recklessness, ending his life prematurely. He clearly had been of no mind to listen to her. His bitter resentment of her and Diego undoubtedly stemmed from a blind and treacherous pride that would not allow him to see her as other than a traitor to her race. That Sheila could have actually preferred Diego to him had both shocked and hurt him. But more than anything, it had infuriated him. His words wounded her very soul, and she would never forget them. She shuddered to think what would have happened had Diego not arrived when he did.

The irony of the whole thing was that Brad, in his searing jealousy, knew what she'd kept denying to herself: she loved Diego. Regardless of her guilty conscience, the fact was inescapable. So was the fact that he remained engaged. This was not some melodrama in which the theme was "love conquers all." This was real life in a highly class-conscious society where tradition, honor and loyalty to family were deeply embedded. What if, for some unknown reason, he did decide to marry his fiancée after all? Would she be able to face the consequences of loving him – the pain of losing him, never seeing him again? Well, if she were being honest with herself, he had never really been hers to lose.

In a fog of despondency, she knelt by her bed that night, praying that whatever the emotional cost to herself, God's will be done. Yet those words seemed empty. She wanted Diego to find a way to break his engagement, find a way to come to her openly without thought of anything but the life that they could build together. But the engagement was not the only thing hampering them. There was the security situation, his wealth being a magnet for terrorists and, more immediately, that rumbling cough in his chest. Was it merely a cold or something more serious?

She rose from her knees. She needed full nights of sleep if she was going to leave her office well organized for her successor, finish culling her possessions, pack up, and fly home to DC. Once again, she would have to confront her mother's blistering criticism about the way she parented Kevin. Then there was the possibility of undergoing language and cultural training at the Foreign Service Institute, depending on what her next assignment would be. How was she going to get through it all? It was then she remembered a scripture – Philippians 4:13, "I can do all things through Christ who strengthens me." She fell asleep as soon as her head touched the pillow.

Strangely or not, Diego would rely on that same verse as he recovered from the infection in his lungs and, once again, prepared to confront not only his father but his fiancée, Rosa Galán.

****

The arrival of Brad Davis's parents in Colombia was, understandably, a solemn occasion. They were escorted by Sam Sheridan of Security from El Dorado Airport to the Hilton Hotel. They came to Bogotá at the personal invitation of Ambassador Váldez who would preside over a memorial tribute to their son before transporting his body back home to New Jersey. At the Ambassador's request, Administrative Officer John Thompson sang the Lord's Prayer in English and its equivalent in Spanish, his rich baritone stirring Davis's mother to tears.

To the surprise of all the staff, Brad Davis's father was an ordained bishop of the Holiness Church. Most of those in attendance were dreading a long-winded sermon full of fiery dogma. To their relief, that did not happen. Bishop Davis began by expressing his and his wife's gratitude for the "many kindnesses" shown them by the Ambassador and the embassy staff as a whole. His ensuing remarks were brief, as were the scriptural passages that he chose to quote, one most notably from Psalm 30 – "Weeping may endure for the night, but joy comes in the morning." As usual at such gatherings, no one said anything negative about the deceased, although his personal reputation was well known. Professionally, however, there was plenty that they could praise, and they did so generously. The memorial tribute ended with Thompson's moving rendition of "Steal Away," a Negro spiritual. As everyone was exiting the auditorium, another surprise came as a young Colombian staffer, Carla Campos, approached the grieving parents, not only to offer her condolences but undoubtedly, by her gestures, to divulge the news of her obvious pregnancy. Witt Jones was on hand to escort the three of them to the Executive Office as speculation swirled among the remaining staff who had witnessed the encounter.

CHAPTER 28

Sheila was glad that she lived in one of the quieter neighborhoods of the capital city, away from the bustling thoroughfare of Santa Bárbara, where the late Brad Davis had had his apartment and where several of the US staff resided. For the two weeks before Christmas, that neighborhood became a hub of fun-loving teenage boys. Of course, their idea of "fun" was quite different from the adult residents who had to endure firecrackers being tossed onto pedestrian walkways day and night. Cynthia Nelson, Personal Assistant to the Ambassador, was one of four direct-hire Americans who submitted written complaints to the RSO which, in turn, notified local police who did nothing. The "fun" didn't stop until Christmas Eve when many families attended holiday mass.

Christmas Eve was memorable for Sheila because at the Bogotá Baptist Chapel's special service, Diego showed up. Pat and Liz were there too and didn't fail to notice him approaching Sheila as most of the congregation headed for refreshments in the church's fellowship hall.

"Diego, what are you doing here? You know we're not supposed to –" Sheila began.

"I must speak with you," he said, gently pulling her toward a side room which Sheila recognized as the choir's robing room. Fortunately, no one was in there.

"It's good to see that you've recovered from that hacking cough. I was worried --"

"Sheila, thank you for your concern, but I would not have come without good reason. Let me explain as quickly as I can, then I will leave," he said, an urgency she'd not heard in his voice since he'd asked her to intervene in the Paul Landers' health incident.

"I believe that I am being followed or my telephone monitored by Galán's private investigator."

"Investigator?" Sheila began before being shushed.

"I have no proof. It is just a — how do you say? -- *hunch*."

"Diego, he may know about us."

"He does know, and I cannot risk your exposure to possible scandal by your continuing association with me."

He took a small pad and pen from his inner pocket and asked her to write down her contact information in the US in case he might not see her again before her Spring departure. She did as she was told, then raised fearful eyes to his face.

"You're saying that we won't even be talking on the phone anymore?"

"That is exactly what I am saying -- until I know more — or something happens."

"I'm afraid that something *will* happen. I was so glad to see you, Diego. I thought —" she hesitated.

"You thought what, my love?"

"That you had – had somehow – found a way to –"

"Not yet. Once again, I must ask for your trust and your patience," he said, pulling her into his arms and holding her in silence. Just then, they heard voices on the other side of the choir's robing room door. Diego silently mouthed, *I love you*, then motioned for her to open the door. She glanced back as she opened the door, but he apparently had disappeared, perhaps hiding himself in a closet or behind a bunch of floor-length robes.

"Sheila! We wondered where you were." Two of the choir members stood there with widened eyes, still wearing their red holiday robes with white collars. Sheila instantly recognized the grey-haired pair from the choir's alto section. Gail was Canadian. Sophie was Haitian.

"Oh, hi, Gail! Hello, Sophie! I must have gotten turned around. That's the robing room," Sheila said, hoping that she sounded convincing.

"Yes, it is. No Christmas goodies in there," Sophie said laughingly.

"Better hurry. Somebody brought plum pudding, and it's going fast!" Gail said.

"Right. Merry Christmas!"

"Happy Christmas!" the pair chorused.

When Sheila entered the crowded fellowship hall, it was as if her boss and his wife had been watching the entryway. For she had taken no more than two steps when Pat said, "Merry Christmas, Sheila! Where's your friend?"

"M-my friend?" she stammered, then exclaimed, "Oh! My *friend!* He, he couldn't stay. He just wanted to – to –"

"Wish you 'Happy Holidays', I'm sure," Pat said, then pointing toward the tables, letting out a chuckle that was anything but jovial, "That's quite a spread, isn't it? The Chapel really knows how to celebrate the holidays!"

"And that music was divine!" enthused Liz. "I never get tired of Handel's 'Messiah'."

"Neither do I," Sheila said, more relaxed as she realized that Liz was clearly unaware of any tension between her husband and Sheila.

"I didn't see you on the security van. Who brought you here?" Pat asked as if warning her to give a straight answer.

"I came with John Thompson on one of the other vans," Sheila said. That was true. She saw John now, holding a plate of uneaten snacks as people surrounded him, obviously to congratulate him on his performance with the choir.

"I think I'll grab a plate before all the good stuff is gone. Merry Christmas, you two! See you in the office next Monday, Pat!" she said as she turned away.

"Count on it," Pat intoned.

Half an hour later, she and John were leaving the church.

"I'm surprised you ever got permission to drive to church," he said.

"There aren't that many of us from the States, although the Pastor is. It's an international fellowship."

"Who was your friend?" he asked as the chauffeur drove toward Sheila's apartment.

Oh, Lord! Did everybody and his brother notice Diego speaking to her?

"That was Dr. Diego Santos. He – he couldn't stay."

"Anything you want to tell me?" John asked.

"If you mean *confide*, I don't think we know each other *that* well."

"Meaning mind my own business, right?"

"I'm sorry. I didn't mean it that way. It's just that I'm tired. I'm tired of all the security – though necessary."

"Who isn't? Well, you'll be out of here sooner than some of us. I wish you a less stressful next assignment," John remarked.

"Thank you. I hear that you once toured the European opera circuit. Do you ever think of doing that again?"

"No. I love singing, but there's no stability in that field unless you're willing to give it one hundred percent. Opera was more my wife's passion than mine, God rest her soul. I'm content in the Foreign Service."

The conversation was easy after that, and ten minutes later, they were dropping her off at her building. Sheila said goodnight and ran into the lobby. As usual, the doorman doffed his cap and summoned the elevator.

CHAPTER 29

How long Christy's pursuit of Diego would have continued is unknown. Nevertheless, a singular event intervened to end her efforts. A triple assassination occurred on a main boulevard in the capital city of Bogotá: the murders of a man posing as Sancho Galán-Garza, the impostor's chauffeur-bodyguard, and Fabio Santos-Lopez. Two other bodyguards were wounded, one critically. According to newspaper accounts, one of Fabio Santos's sons had recently married the daughter of the cartel boss posing as Galán. The question arose as to whether or not she too was an impostor. Still another issue was how active the groom was in the cartel. As far as Christy was concerned, it didn't matter that the criminal was now dead. Diego Santos was no longer of interest to her. His engagement announcement had been big news in the society pages last year, but now that he had actually married into a crime family, regardless of *how* physically attractive he was, she couldn't afford to even flirt with him, never mind sleep with him. Some men simply were not worth the risk – not when her career was at stake.

****

Political Counselor Patrick Carmichael, Regional Security Officer Witt Jones, and Drug Enforcement Special Agent Tyrone "Ty"

Collier met in Jones's office to discuss the facts surrounding their latest coordinated case. Collier, a street-savvy agent who was rising steadily in the ranks, was a muscular Black man of medium height and hue, whose rugged looks women found attractive. He, however, wasn't cut from the same cloth as Brad Davis. Totally devoted to his wife and infant twin boys, he was equally devoted to his work and left no one in doubt of it. He had requested this meeting today, and Carmichael's deep blue eyes shone with appreciation for Collier's strictly-business demeanor.

There presently was no direct threat to embassy personnel, but an article in *El Tiempo*, the main city newspaper, woke them up to the fact that Sheila Dunbar, most likely unknowingly, had associated with a man linked to the former drug cartel boss, Pedro Guzman-Negrino, alias Sancho Galán-Garza. Of course, she was now out of any potential danger. Carmichael and Jones had seen to that. Three days after Christmas, they had put her on a flight to DC. For, after Santos brazenly contacted Sheila at the Chapel's Christmas Eve service, they realized that he was not only risking his own life, but hers also. That was two months ago. They hadn't even given Sheila a chance to pack more than what she could carry in three suitcases. The Embassy's General Services Office supervised the crating of her HHE (household effects) and had them shipped to a government warehouse in Maryland. Sheila had since received notice of her next assignment, Paris, and could arrange for them to be shipped there once she finished her training at the Foreign Service Institute in Arlington, Virginia.

Pat felt badly about the whole thing. Sheila was an excellent officer manager, and the temporary duty employee sent to hold down the fort in the Political Section couldn't hold a candle to her in efficiency, but it had to be done. Fortunately, there had been only a few more months on Sheila's tour of duty, but Pat simply hated the way she had to leave – being rushed away from post as if Santos's actions were somehow *her* fault. Oh, well, it was neither here nor there, as they say. Their focus had to be on any fallout from these latest assassinations. Guzman-Negrino hadn't been the biggest cartel head, but he had been one of the most powerful.

Despite his lack of a formal education, Guzman had a knack for making money. He was clever, cunning, even brilliant, and, when he deemed it necessary, ruthless. His school had been the streets of Medellín where, as a half-starving urchin forced by his parents to steal, he'd learned the art of survival and had his first contact with drugs. A lucrative business in cocaine had flourished into an empire, and then *El Jefe* (the boss), as he was widely known, played it smart. He began investing his drug money in legitimate enterprises. While Fabio Santos stuck with textiles, Guzman diversified. His fortune ballooned beyond his highest expectations. A couple of years ago, he had disappeared from Medellín and gone respectable, relocating to the Colombian capital and living as Sancho Galán-Garza. He'd been clean since then and had broken his *Mafiosa* ties. Yet the past had a long shadow, and he would never feel safe or be the equal of an educated, high-class Colombian society.

Guzman needed a name, a connection that would open doors for him, admit him to the circles of the elite whose snubs he'd endured for decades. Despite Guzman's efforts to shed his criminal image, it was an open secret that the drug-crime world had a code of payback, which was not always immediate but always inevitable.

El Tiempo printed a graphic account of the murders, accompanied by sobering photographs of the bloody aftermath. Unfortunately, Fabio Santos and the bodyguards were expendable simply because they were with Guzman. The article stated that the exact motive for the crime was unknown but was probably revenge-related. The article took on a philosophical bent by stating that nothing in this world was guaranteed. For who would have imagined that the happy occasions of an engagement and wedding would be eclipsed by the planning of a funeral for Fabio Santos, one of the city's most prestigious residents? It ended with the well-worn phrase, *"Así es la vida."*

Así es la vida – Such is life. Witt Jones was stroking his chin in bewilderment.

"Usually, these high-society weddings make front-page headlines. Our Press Officer located last year's engagement announcement in *Cromos* magazine, but she couldn't confirm that it actually culminated in a wedding between Dr. Diego Santos and Rosa Galán. Of course, it could have been a small, intimate ceremony."

"Probably was. Guzman wouldn't have wanted to draw too much attention to the wedding and, thus, himself," Ty Collier noted.

"The big question is how Guzman managed to pull off the ruse for so long. His face should have been instantly recognizable," Pat wondered aloud.

"You underestimate the resourcefulness of these drug lords," Ty commented. "The real Sancho Galán-Garza is dead. His body and those of his wife and daughter were discovered in a grave on his former coffee plantation outside Medellín a week ago. From what one of our sources tell us — and we've corroborated this — things were getting pretty hot for Guzman-Negrino in Medellín. He needed a new identity to make a fresh start. Galán-Garza made the perfect stand-in. With a little surgical nip and tuck, Guzman assumed Galán's identity; murdered him, his wife, and daughter — or had them murdered; somehow acquired access to enough legal documentation to sell the coffee plantation; and the plan was foolproof — or so he thought."

"Sheila's involvement with Diego Santos didn't help any — as innocent as it was," Pat remarked.

"Who says it was innocent? She admitted to his spending at least one night in her apartment," Witt noted.

"She admitted it and explained it," Pat noted.

"She did, and you believed her," Witt countered in a cynical tone.

"Hey, guys! She's left post. The point should be moot by now," Ty intervened.

"But, is it?" Witt asked. "What if they're still in touch with each other?"

"What if — for now — we focus on the facts surrounding Guzman and Rosa?" Ty stated, emphasizing "Rosa" with imaginary two-fingered quote marks on each raised hand.

"Okay," Witt said with a nod. "We know that 'Rosa' wasn't — isn't her real name and that she wasn't his -- daughter." His salacious tone had Pat's full attention.

"Are you saying --?" Pat began.

"You got it," Witt broke in. "The pretty *señorita* reportedly was Guzman's mistress, but that's quite a stretch considering his age and, according to the grapevine, his impotence. Hair dye and cosmetic surgery can do only so much. The man was seventy years old, trying to project fifty-five. More than likely, he himself spread the tale. What is it with these guys and their colossal egos?"

Pat and Ty cast glances of irony in Witt's direction without commenting.

Ty continued, "Speaking of tales, the older woman, his cousin, was acting the part of his — that is, Galán-Garza's wife. We understand that she's a genius with makeup. As for the fair Rosa, we believe he picked her up after the murders were committed. Her true name is Elena Pacheco. She comes from a respectable but poor family in Medellín that seems to have been clueless as to the true identity of their -- *benefactor.* In any case, with this marriage, Elena and her family have moved several rungs up the social ladder."

"My head is spinning," Pat commented.

"As well it should be," Witt stated. "Let's just hope that Sheila's absence hasn't caused Santos's heart to grow fonder and that the affair between them is over."

"Witt, if by *affair*, you mean some sordid indulgence of the senses, you don't know Sheila. She's not that type," Pat protested.

"Oh, Pat, me lad! *All* women are *that* type," Witt drawled with a touch of the burr on his tongue.

"Hey, guys," Ty intervened again. "I can assure you that there has been no evidence of telephone contact since Sheila left. Don't look at me like that, Pat. We have the full cooperation of Colombian authorities. They placed the wire taps on Santos's residence and office phone lines. We got a lead that he's living with a colleague, so they tapped that line too. No nibbles yet."

"That doesn't mean that all our bases are covered. What if they're writing to each other?" Witt asked.

"We haven't yet gotten the go-ahead to request a mail intercept. Seems the Colombians are already stretched thin," Ty said.

"Don't you think this could be a bit of overkill? There's no evidence that Dr. Santos or his father was involved in any drug trade activities, is there? It appears that both were totally ignorant of Guzman-Negrino's true identity. Right?" Pat remarked.

"I'll give you that," Ty replied.

"On the other hand," Witt said, "you know what a stickler the Ambassador is for policy *and* appearances. Even a whiff of an embassy staffer's connection to Guzman could be bad news."

"It could negatively impact Sheila's career," Pat remarked.

"Or worse, hurt our image as crime fighters on the front lines of the drug war. Are you sure, Carmichael, that this thing between Sheila and Diego Santos is over?" Ty asked.

"I think so," Pat replied.

"Better make sure," Witt advised.

"You mean ... snoop?" Pat said, a look of distaste on his face.

"No, no," Witt instantly assured him. "Just call her. Ask her if he's been in touch with her. Appeal to her ... Christian values. After all, adultery is a sin, isn't it?"

"Adultery? Come on!" Pat exclaimed, still indignant over the recent false accusation against him and Sheila. "I won't do it!"

"OK," Witt said with a shrug. "Have it your way, but sooner or later, someone will have to do it. Think it over, Carmichael. If this thing starts to blow up in our faces, don't say I didn't warn you."

"Blow up? Please spare me the drama!"

"No drama — just making sure there are no barking dogs running loose out there that could come back to bite us. Think it over," Witt said in a casual — too casual — tone. "And don't forget to make it official — on a secure line."

Collier and Jones gave him a knowing look as he left the Security Office. Thinking over the warning, Pat later changed his mind about calling Sheila.

****

It was eight in the evening in DC. Sheila had had an intense day of training at the Foreign Service Institute, being enrolled in a French course that required total immersion into the language. In other words, after the first day, neither the students nor the instructors were allowed to speak any English in class. That was why it was critical to study the thick language manual; tune into France 2 on television for the news in French; and listen to broadcasts in French on the radio. It helped that Washington, DC, being our nation's capital, is a city of many embassies and legations. Perhaps only the United Nations headquarters in Geneva, Switzerland, and the UN in New York City host more diplomats. So, there were no barriers to accessing foreign languages — and no excuses for not doing so.

Sheila had kissed Kevin good night after reading the story of *Daniel in the Lion's Den* and was reviewing exercises in the French manual for the next class when the phone rang.

"I'll get it. You keep studying," her mother said, picking up the phone in the kitchen. She was relieved that since her daughter was unwilling to give up what Dorothy termed the "gypsy life", she at least had been given a "decent" assignment. Dorothy Dunbar could already picture herself at the Eiffel Tower or a sidewalk café, eating a rich chocolate mousse. She had long dreamed of vacationing in Paris.

Whomever she was expecting at the other end of the line, it certainly wasn't Sheila's former boss.

"It's Mr. Carmichael!" she shouted. "Pick it up in there."

While Sheila and her mother had declared a truce since she got home (mainly because of her upcoming Paris assignment), Dorothy was never one to be left out of the loop regarding anything to do with her daughter's life. So, she had no qualms about listening in on the kitchen phone when Sheila answered on the extension. It didn't occur to her that eavesdropping was a clandestine form of digging. All she could think about was getting to the bottom of whatever Sheila was involved in because whatever it was, it would eventually end up affecting Kevin too. She listened intently and hung up in frustration when Sheila's boss advised that they would need to speak on one of the State Department's secure lines because what he had to say was classified. They agreed on a time the next day and a place where they could speak freely. The only thing of interest that Dorothy could glean was that it was about "a mutual friend." Dorothy would bide her time, even if impatiently. She already had *some* information, but "by hook or by crook" she intended to find out what was behind that phone call, or her name wasn't Dorothy Janelle Jackson Dunbar!

* *

Sheila arranged to be transported from the training institute to Department of State headquarters during her lunch hour. She was escorted to a room where a secure telephone was available. Within five minutes, Pat called. She began the conversation with an attempt at levity.

"Pat, I know I'm indispensable, but at least give my replacement a chance!"

"I'm afraid this is no laughing matter," Pat said in a grave tone.

"What's happened?" Sheila asked.

"First, I want you to know I'm sorry we had to cut your tour short, but your association with Dr. Santos –"

"It's okay, Pat. It was time and, believe me, I was ready to go. If this is about the assassination of the doctor's father and the man posing as a coffee plantation owner, it's made international headlines."

"I figured you'd know that by now, but –" Pat hesitated.

"There's more than what's been in the news?"

"I think you should know that Colombian authorities, at our – at Security's request, have been electronically monitoring the doctor. Before you say anything, I want you to know that through those wiretaps, they determined that neither the doctor nor his father had any idea of the drug lord's true identity. They assumed that he was who he said he was. So, your *friend* has been cleared of suspicion in that regard."

"I must say that I'm happy to hear it," Sheila stated.

"Well, don't get too happy. I'm actually calling on behalf of the RSO and the DEA. They're asking that if the doctor has been in touch with you, by *whatever* means – and we know it hasn't been by telephone – at least not by the lines being monitored -- that you cut off any and all contact with him."

"Why? From this distance, what possible --"

"Does that mean the two of you have been communicating?"

"Yes, but not lately. I wrote him about getting my assignment to Paris. He wrote back congratulating me and saying that he would soon have good news to share."

"Was it about his engagement?"

"I – assumed it would be."

"Were you aware that Santos was engaged to be married when you were seeing him?"

"Please, Pat. You make it sound like something illicit was going on. He told me that he was engaged – unhappily engaged – and that he wanted to get out of it."

"Well, if the main newspaper here is accurate, he didn't – get out of it, I mean. To put it bluntly, your involvement with Diego Santos puts the embassy in a rather precarious position."

"My involvement? He's there. I'm here. I haven't heard from him in a while, and I don't expect to ever again -- because of his -- marriage." The sadness in her voice was unmistakable.

"Which is no guarantee that he won't try to contact you again – even if it's not to resume a – a friendship with you. You see, Santos's father was murdered because he happened to be in the wrong place at the wrong time. As I mentioned before, there's no evidence that he was ever mixed up in the drug trade. However, the man posing as Sancho Galán-Garza, the respectable coffee farmer, was an ex-big-time narcotrafficker named Pedro Guzman-Negrino. Extraditing traffickers is the top priority of the US Mission here, Sheila. Now, if we've got an employee connected even remotely with Guzman's son-in-law —"

"But he wasn't Guzman's son-in-law when I was seeing him!"

"I know. Santos may be clean, but mud sticks by association. If he contacts you again, and the press, either ours or Colombia's, gets wind of your involvement with him, past or present, it could complicate that extradition treaty."

"Let me get this straight, Pat. Diego — Dr. Santos married Guzman's daughter. Now, by association, he's being painted with the same broad brush as his late father-in-law."

"Exactly."

"And even my past association with Dr. Santos could lead to a lot of speculation and people jumping to the wrong conclusions that would reflect negatively on the embassy and its mission."

"I couldn't have explained it better myself. There's no doubt that he was engaged while he was seeing you. You could plead ignorance on that score, but it might not sound credible."

"I told you. I knew he was engaged. He didn't try to deceive me."

"And yet you still maintained a liaison with him."

"Liaison? Pat, that has a nasty ring to it. When did he get married?" Sheila asked, the tightness in her throat making it difficult for her to get the words out.

"We don't know. *El Tiempo* reported it as recent. *Cromos* magazine carried the engagement announcement last year, so it's not like the marriage was unexpected. The bottom line, Sheila, is that you've got to cut any and all ties to Dr. Santos. If he contacts you, tell him that as a Christian, you can't have a relationship with a married man. He'll get it. It's not just for building diplomatic relations and stemming the drug war, Sheila. This could follow you to your next assignment, hurt your chances for promotion. Do I have your word that you'll do the right thing?"

"Yes, Pat. You've made your point. Be assured that the embassy has nothing to concern itself about. Now, I need to get back to my French class, *s'il te plaît.*"

Pat let out an audible sigh of relief, told her how much he appreciated the work she'd done in the Political Section, and remarked that since the Christmas Eve service at the Chapel, he and Liz had gone to a few of the Sunday services.

"I'm so glad, Pat!"

They hung up on a cordial note, and Sheila returned to her French class, exhilarated about Pat and Liz's decision to attend services at the Chapel. Yet even this good news was dampened by the fact that Diego was married. That, of course, was why she hadn't heard from him for a while – and certainly never would again.

She went home that evening with a heavy heart. This was the price she had hoped she'd never have to pay -- losing what she'd never truly had. The pain of never seeing him again was a hard thing to endure. She picked at the meal her mother had prepared, then announced that she was going to bed as soon as Kevin was tucked in for the night.

No sooner had Sheila whispered a quick prayer and slid under the bed covers than a tap on the door was followed without pause by her mother entering. She stood over the bed and asked, "Is there something you're not telling me, Sheila Marie?"

Sheila realized that her mother was about to embark on a *digging* expedition. For she seldom addressed Sheila by her middle name unless she wanted something – and meant to get it.

"Mama, I can't talk about it," she said.

"You mean *him*, don't you? Mr. Carmichael mentioned a mutual friend."

"So, you were listening."

Dorothy nodded and pursed her lips.

"Our further conversation was confidential. I'm not at liberty to discuss it."

"Well, I have a feeling that it's about a *man* – some Latino you got entangled with down in that place. Am I right?"

"Mama, it's over."

"Uh-huh. But you've been moping around here for weeks now. Are *you* over *him?*"

"I'd rather not talk about it," Sheila said.

"Have it your way. Just remember that your son *must* come first."

And with that, Dorothy left her alone with her misery. For Sheila definitely wasn't over him and wondered if she ever would be. In the darkness of her room, she prayed, "Oh, Lord, I'm weak. I can't get through this without You. Help me. Please help me!"

At that moment, peacefulness enveloped her, and she drifted off into dreamless slumber.

* *

In her own bedroom, Dorothy was unlocking the upper partition of her roll-top desk. From one of the cubbies, she took out four envelopes bearing foreign postage. She had watched for and met the mailman each day, gone through the mail and placed the various pieces on a tray in the front hall – all except what she held in her hands now. As she'd slipped them into the bodice of her dress, she'd felt uneasy about confiscating mail addressed to her daughter but gradually pushed her hesitation aside to read the contents of each letter. The last letter shared the news of a broken engagement. Well, she was no fool! The name *Santos* in the return address and in the international news reports exposed the lie. That Latino was trifling! There *had* been a wedding, a recent wedding, and it had taken a news report to bring Sheila to her senses! It was obvious that she was heartbroken, but over time she'd get over it.

Dorothy thought about burning the letters, but decided against it – in case she needed some ammunition to confront this "Diego" directly – which she doubted would ever happen. But if it did, she'd be ready. *The dog, the spineless dog!* She replaced the letters in the cubby, pulled down the roll-top and relocked the desk. She too prayed that night – for strength to do what was best for her daughter and grandson.

CHAPTER 30

How her mother had deduced so much from overhearing the phrase "our mutual friend" was a mystery to Sheila. But, like a dog digging up a bone, she was fiercely determined to extract as much information as she could from her daughter. So, the relentless probing began: "Just who is this 'mutual friend'? A Colombian doctor? A Christian, you say? Or is he simply wearing the label? Well, behavior is what counts." She quoted Matthew 7:16, "You will know them by their fruits."

When Sheila avoided divulging the confidential elements of her conversation with Pat, her mother soon found another topic of interest.

"You aren't very savvy where men are concerned, are you?"

Sheila felt like screaming. Instead, she took a deep breath and remarked, "Mama, I don't see what difference it makes at this point."

"It doesn't – unless he calls again. He did call last night, didn't he?"

"Yes, but as you know – after all, you answered the phone – I refused to talk to him."

"That was the sensible thing to do because that fine Black MD at church is just waiting for his chance —"

"I'm not interested," Sheila broke in.

"Why not? No, don't answer that. I know there are Afro-Latinos. This Diego. Is he one of those?"

"I don't think so, but I couldn't care less."

"For the sake of Kevin's future, you *should* care. There's no substitute for a Black man's influence on the life of a Black boy. Think about it."

Sheila *had* thought about it. She knew her mother's point was valid, and she meant well. However, love couldn't be turned off like a spigot. Since the news of Diego's wedding, she'd tried to push him out of her thoughts. She'd studied hard and earned a high score on her latest French exam. A day of shopping at Woodie's netted a dozen outfits, ten of which she ended up returning. Being a DC native, she was familiar with the Smithsonian museums, the National Zoo, Mount Vernon, and Williamsburg, plus many of the monuments. With Kevin in tow, she spent her Saturdays touring them again. All that activity only increased her longing for outings with Diego. Worship services at the Shiloh Baptist Church were as spirited as ever. Lively gospel songs ascended to the rafters, and the pastor, with his energetic preaching, had many of those in attendance clapping and enthusiastically responding, "Amen!" To her mother's dismay, Sheila sat in the padded pew, stoic and silent, seemingly in a world of her own.

Sheila prolonged Kevin's bedtimes by reading more than one story; tried baking new recipes; and telephoned Cynthia Nelson in Bogotá to chat. Yet, the false front of cheerfulness she daily tried to project was beginning to slip.

Diego suspected surveillance by a private investigator, but that hadn't stopped him from calling her again, apparently from some unknown safe place. In any case, she had nothing to say to him now that he was married. As difficult as it was, the next time he called, Sheila cut him off abruptly. "Don't call me again, Diego."

"Sheila, please. I wish to explain –"

"It's over!" she hissed into the phone, slammed down the receiver and retreated to her bedroom, devastated. Even had she not been asked to cut all ties with him, she knew that it was necessary. He was married, lost to her forever, and he hadn't respected her enough to come clean about the wedding. Instead, he'd raised her hopes and made her believe that there was a chance for them to – what? He'd written two letters and then stopped – as if he suddenly forgot her existence. She wasn't falling for some lame-brained *explanation*!

A third telephone call came a week later – not from Diego, but from someone calling himself Dr. Suárez. She remembered Diego mentioning renting a room in his house. The doctor identified himself as Diego's friend and said he was calling on his behalf. At that point, Sheila frostily informed him that Dr. Santos was no longer of any interest to her, adding, "Please advise your friend not to *ever* contact me again."

"But –"

She hung up the phone.

As was her habit these days, she retreated to the solitude of her bedroom, finally giving in to the deep sadness over her failed efforts to banish Diego from her thoughts, from her heart. Sobs wracked her body, shaking her to the very core of her being.

Kevin's voice penetrated her anguish. He was in the kitchen, loudly proclaiming, "I don't want an apple, Grandma. I want ice cream!"

Sheila quickly got up, wiped her eyes with a tissue, and hurried into the kitchen, where Dorothy was opening the freezer section of the refrigerator.

"Mr. Kevin Horne. You know the rule: Dessert after, not before, dinner. If you're hungry, eat an apple for now," Sheila said.

"I'm not hungry," he said in a grumbling tone. "I just want some ice cream."

"What did I say?" Sheila asked him. When he didn't answer, she said, "Come here, son."

She put an arm around him and said, "After dinner, you may have ice cream. Do you know what self-control is?"

He nodded.

"Well, big boys have self-control. They know how to wait. Can you wait?"

"Yes," he replied, almost grudgingly.

"I'm proud of you, son. Did the teacher give you any homework for the weekend?"

"Uh-huh. I have to practice addition and read a book. Addition is fun, but that book is stupid!"

"I don't believe your teacher would place something stupid in your class's library. Perhaps it's just not much fun. Can you think of another word to describe it?"

Kevin slanted his head and thought for a second before saying, "It's silly."

"May I see the book?" Sheila asked.

He pulled his backpack off, unzipped a side pocket, and drew out a thin illustrated hardcover titled *The Sky Is Falling!*

Sheila smiled. "I read this when I was your age! Chicken Little, Henny Penny —"

"Goosey Lucy, Turkey Lurkey, and Foxy Loxy," Kevin finished with a sneer. "We read that when I was in kindergarten. I'm six!"

"Maybe some of your classmates haven't yet read it. Who chose the book for you?"

"Nobody. By the time I got to the bookcase, it was what was left. It's — silly," he repeated. "Everybody knows animals can't talk!"

"Not like people, but in their own way, they can. It's been a long time since I've heard that story. Why don't you read it for me now? Then, you do your addition, and after dinner and ice cream, we'll read a bedtime Bible story."

Kevin's eyes lit up. "Which one, Mom?"

"It'll be a surprise, Sweet Pea."

"Oh, Mom, I'm too old for that."

"The story?" she asked, suppressing a grin.

"No. That Sweet Pea stuff."

After Kevin read *The Sky Is Falling*, Sheila gave him a hug and said, "I know you're a big boy now, so I'll expect big-boy behavior. Promise?"

"I'll do my best, Mom," he said, sitting down at the kitchen table to eagerly tackle his addition exercises.

They had just finished placing dishes into the dishwasher when the phone rang. Dorothy answered it. "Sheila, it's for you."

Sheila shook her head and told Kevin, "Get ready. The surprise story is coming up."

Kevin headed for his room. Again, Sheila shook her head.

"It's Robert," Dorothy told her.

Relieved that it wasn't Diego calling again, but irritated at the prospect of talking to her ex-husband, she took the receiver and asked, "What do you want, Robert?"

"Nice to hear your voice too, Sheila," Robert remarked sarcastically.

"Unless it concerns Kevin, I'm not in the mood. So, get to the point!" she snapped.

"It's not about Kevin."

"Then, goodbye, Robert."

"Don't hang up! Listen, Sheila, I need to see you!"

The urgency in his voice failed to move her.

"About what?"

"Tanya and I are … going our separate ways. She's filed for divorce."

"And you thought I would care."

"I *hoped* you would care because of what we once had."

"Robert, what we once had was a mockery of the word *marriage*, and you know it."

"I messed up big-time," he admitted. "But I never stopped loving you, Sheila. Can you ever forgive me?"

"I already did."

"Good. I know I don't deserve a second chance but if you're willing, I swear I'll prove —"

"Prove it to your wife, Robert. She's the one you need to convince – not me. Goodnight!"

She hung up the phone, exclaimed "Men!" in disgust, and headed for Kevin's bedroom.

When she announced the surprise story as *David and Goliath*, he shouted, "Bring it on, Mom!"

"I guess it's not a surprise. Do you already know the story?"

"Yes, from Sunday School, but it's my favorite. Everyone but David was afraid of the giant from Palestine, but David took him down with just one rock in his slingshot."

"That's right, except the giant was a Philistine," Sheila corrected him, "and David was brave because he did it in the name of –"

She paused, and Kevin shouted, "The Lord!"

"That's right. Why don't we share the reading? You read a page, then I'll read a page. Okay?"

By the time the story ended, Sheila's mood had lightened.

"I love you, Mom," Kevin said as she adjusted his pillow, hugged him, and kissed his forehead.

"I love you more, Sweet Pea," she said. This time he didn't protest. His eyelids were already drooping as she pulled the bedcovers up to his chin.

She returned to the kitchen to find her mother sitting at the table working on a word-search puzzle.

"Are you waiting up for me?" Sheila asked.

"That's right. I must say I'm glad you're not getting involved with Robert. He had a good thing and ruined it."

"But you were against my divorcing him despite his cheating," Sheila reminded her.

"Yes, because I thought that sooner or later, he would come to his senses – which he did, but too late. If he can, he ought to work things out with his wife, not come running back to you like a whipped puppy."

"Mama, thank you for supporting me," Sheila quietly commented.

"Well, right is right, and wrong is wrong," Dorothy staunchly declared.

She stood up, said "Sleep well," and left for bed with her head held high.

Sheila turned out the kitchen light and headed down the hall, wondering if she had merely imagined that her mother's judgmental tone was also meant for *her*.

****

As dawn broke the next morning, a low malevolent cackle emanated from a shadowy corner of Sheila's bedroom. *Juan!* Sheila bolted upright in bed, eyes wide open and darting around the room, pulses racing, then settling as she confirmed that no one was there. Then, a sweet whisper brought comfort to her soul: "I will never leave you nor forsake you." A holy scripture, a promise to God's people, spoken long ago by an Old Testament prophet, but now voiced by another: Diego. Diego, the man she had loved, *still* loved. That same voice asked, "Do you trust me?" She swallowed hard and answered with a resounding "No!" into the gaping emptiness of her heart.

Swinging her legs over the side of the bed, Sheila stood and stretched upward, speaking words of faith aloud: "My God, I trust in You – in You alone."

CHAPTER 31

"**W**hat!" Dorothy exclaimed.

"I'm not going to Paris," Sheila repeated.

"You finally get the assignment of your dreams, and now you don't want it?"

"Not my dreams, Mama. Yours."

Dorothy was baffled but managed to find her voice. "I admit that a month in Paris, while you and Kevin settled in, was pretty appealing to me. Now you're not going. What happened?"

"I've been approved for a position at headquarters. Fortunately, my household effects are still in the Maryland warehouse. Mama, I thought you'd be jumping for joy. You never approved of what you call my gypsy lifestyle."

"Because of Kevin, but who wouldn't want to go to Paris?"

I don't, not anymore! Sheila silently replied. She might have laughed if the situation weren't so ironic. Her mother had been brimming with enthusiasm over her Paris assignment while she had lost all interest in it. Once, any assignment offering Sheila the opportunity to acquire new language skills and learn about new cultures would have been a dream come true in the very competitive ranks of the State Department's Foreign Service

Corps. This upcoming transfer to the State Department's Civil Service would place her exactly where her mother used to say she belonged – in a permanent DC position. Her zest for living abroad had greatly diminished, if not altogether vanished. The years stretched ahead, colorless and meaningless, all because of one man – a man she must forget or never know peace of mind again. And by the mercy of God, she would!

Her headquarters assignment would provide the financial stability she needed for a new career eventually. Apart from travel, Black history and culture remained one of her few lifelong interests. So, she'd applied for the Master's degree program in African American Studies at Howard University. However, she had no intention of telling her mother about it unless she was admitted to the program. While approving the area of study, Dorothy would certainly ask what Sheila intended to do with the degree when she got it. Sheila wondered the same thing herself, but she desperately needed that program in order to keep her mind occupied and off Diego.

Sheila sighed. Dorothy thought she knew why, and commented, "Dr. Stone asked why you weren't at church last Sunday."

"Are you referring to the Black MD?"

"None other."

It was a Saturday morning. Kevin and Bobby, one of his neighborhood pals, were in the den watching a *Fat Albert* cartoon on television. By their boyish laughter, they were thoroughly enjoying themselves.

"I'm going to check on the boys," Sheila said.

Dorothy responded with a nod but said nothing. Instead, she was thinking, *Sheila's really trying to get over that Latino, thank God!*

****

Down in Bogotá, Diego Santos and Lorenzo Suárez were having a morning coffee break at the Clínica Palermo.

"You are not serious!" Lorenzo stated, shaking his head.

"I have never been more serious," Diego said. "I leave next Tuesday. She will have been there at least a week. I can hardly wait."

"What if she still refuses to talk with you?"

"I will make her listen – somehow," Diego insisted.

Lorenzo, once again, asked himself if his friend had totally lost his ability to reason but aloud commented, "I hear that Paris is beautiful any season of the year."

Diego seemed lost in thought. Was he already mentally flying across the Atlantic on what was bound to be a hopeless quest? Lorenzo feared that his friend would be hurt and disappointed after so many futile efforts, yet he knew that nothing would deter him. Poor, blind fool!

****

The night before his departure to Paris, Diego slept better than he had in a long time. For over two years, his dreams had been haunted by the face of a young boy – the child whose head had been battered by a stallion, the child he had been unable to save. Then there were the anguished cries of the dying and injured in Armero and Chiva-Chiva, victims of the

Nevado del Ruiz volcanic eruption. Screams of grief and pain by the survivors and their loved ones receded into a muted distance during the day and swelled to high volume in his sleep. Worse was the memory of the dead: smothered faces, broken heads, crushed torsos, limbs at grotesque angles; twisted, bloodied bodies. First responders in hip-high boots, face masks, reflective clothing, special gloves and head gear reaching down, grasping, pulling, retrieving people from the mud, silt, ash, and debris. The responders and aid workers, including his medical team, had been lauded as heroes. He was no hero, Diego told himself. Many people had been rescued, but so many more had perished. Those were the ones he wept over, less often now, but they still lingered in his thoughts daily – the ones he could not save.

That night, however, after a hot shower, a light meal of grilled fish and rice, and a chilled glass of pineapple juice, Diego was full of hope, a hope that not only brought physical renewal to his body but clarity to his mind and lightness to his heart. The only face in his dreams that night was that of Sheila – his beautiful Sheila. Just thinking of her brought a smile to his lips, even as he slept. The day of his arrival would be a workday for her at the US Embassy in Paris. His flight would not arrive before the Embassy closed, but he would be there when it opened on Wednesday morning. Whatever the reason for her rejection of him, he would find out and make everything right between them. He would! He had to!

CHAPTER 32

Sheila was not admitted to Howard University for the fall semester. After all, she had applied at the last minute. These days, she seemed to be simply going through the motions of living. She had turned on the radio that late-Sunday afternoon and heard the voice of Julio Iglesias singing "Hey" in English. The English version of the song was sweet and romantic, while the original Spanish lyrics spoke of deception and unrequited love. There *had* been a sweetness in her and Diego's relationship, but there also had been deception – not solely on his part but also on hers. She had deceived herself into believing that there was a chance of his ending his engagement. For some unknown reason, he had not, and the question of "why" had tormented her ever since she'd seen the article in the newspaper about the assassinations of the drug lord, along with Diego's father, and one of the three bodyguards. Finally, she'd resigned herself to the inevitability of moving on with her life, however dull it had become.

Autumn was her favorite time of year. The brilliant golds, oranges and reds of the foliage had never failed to capture her attention and cause her to marvel at the majesty of God's creation. Yet today, she took no pleasure in the beauties of nature right outside her bedroom window as she reviewed the *Rules of Conduct* manual for her new Civil Service position. Later, she would be busy baking cookies and reading a bedtime Bible story with Kevin but, for the moment, he was out walking Rags, the mutt. Her mother was in the den, probably quilting or knitting. The house seemed eerily silent until the doorbell pealed, stirring her out of her doldrums.

Usually so alert and on top of everything, Dorothy was seated in a rocker in the den. The cool temperatures of autumn would soon give way to winter, so she was knitting a wool navy sweater for Kevin. When the doorbell rang, she thought, *Probably Mr. Atkinson*. He was a widower who was new to the neighborhood. They'd been exchanging stories of their grandchildren's escapades. She kept her seat. It wouldn't do to look overly eager.

Sheila went to the front door and looked through the peephole. The sight of Diego standing there ripped through her emotions like a double-edged dagger. What was this? His idea of a joke? He was married. What, in heaven's name, had possessed him to come here? Well, if he thought she was going to fall into his arms like some infatuated schoolgirl, he was highly mistaken. He rang the doorbell a second time. Willing herself to be calm despite the thumping in her chest, Sheila opened the door. It was then that she saw the flowers, a huge bouquet of pink roses. She spared them one disdainful glance before facing him.

"Well, this is a surprise," she announced, trying to inject a coldness into her voice that she was far from feeling.

"I had to come, Sheila," he said, his tone husky. "I could not come sooner. Perhaps you know — about my father?"

"Yes. My condolences, Diego."

"I suppose it was inevitable. He did not know with whom he was dealing."

Sheila refrained from commenting further. She had never met his father or the man masquerading as Sancho Galán-Garza. Instead, she bluntly demanded, "Why are you here, Diego?"

"We must talk," he said. Then, with the desperation of one at the end of his endurance, he asked, "Must we converse in this doorway?"

Reluctantly, she stepped back and motioned him inside. She led him into the den and introduced him to her mother. By that time, Kevin was seated at her feet, chatting away about his new puppy, Rags.

"Pleased to meet you," Dorothy Dunbar muttered in a tone that sounded anything but pleased. In fact, she resented his presence in her house.

"The pleasure is mine, Mrs. Dunbar," Diego responded. Then, bending to shake Kevin's hand, he smiled and remarked, "And you must be the famous Kevin."

Kevin was rather puzzled but pleased by this descriptor of him. He smiled back and replied, "Yes, sir!"

Sheila frowned and pointed Kevin toward the back door. "Son, would you go out and play with Rags while Dr. Santos and I visit?"

"I just finished walking him, Mom," Kevin said.

"I know, but that puppy needs lots of exercise. While you're out there, give him a bath and brush him. And don't forget the doggie treats under the kitchen sink," she said.

Off Kevin went while Dorothy remained seated, seemingly absorbed in her knitting.

Stammering, Sheila offered him a seat on the sofa, wishing her mother would disappear so that they could get this over with.

Diego sat down, hitching his faultlessly creased trousers. A heavy, uncomfortable silence fell upon the room. Shortly, he stood up, courteously inclined his head, and addressed her mother, "Mrs. Dunbar, would you be so kind as to allow us some time alone?"

"Certainly," came the cool response. However, Dorothy was obviously annoyed by the request, as evidenced by her haughty departure from the room, and despite her offer to place the roses in water.

Diego reseated himself, motioning for Sheila to sit beside him. Instead, she took an adjacent armchair. A wounded look suffused his features, and she almost felt sorry for him. Almost. This was no time to let sympathy overrule common sense. The fact remained: he was married and shouldn't even be here.

"Well?" She prompted.

"Sheila, I thought your next assignment was Paris."

"It was. I changed my mind. I'm assigned here in Washington now."

"As I discovered when I arrived at the embassy."

"You *dared* go to Paris and then come here after all that's happened?" Sheila asked in amazement.

"I would have dared much more than that to be with you." His tone was soft, pleading.

Sheila hardened her own voice. "Well, you're here – not that I care."

His confusion was obvious. "That is why I am here. You *did* care, but something happened. What was it, Sheila?"

She stared at him in disbelief, then took a deep breath before icily stating, "I *thought* you respected me, Diego."

"I did. I do!" he said with an earnestness that she judged to be an excellent effort at acting – a futile effort.

"Yet you married the woman you *claimed* not to love and –"

"I did what!" Diego asked. His shock seemed so genuine that Sheila herself was taken aback – at least momentarily.

"Don't bother trying to explain it away."

"There is nothing to explain away because –"

"On that we can agree!" Sheila snapped.

"Sheila, I broke the engagement. I wrote to you –" he stopped in frustration at her upraised hand.

"Diego, the hole is deep enough. Stop digging," she quietly commanded. She stood up and turned her back on him. He also stood and walked over to place his hands on her shoulders, and felt her stiffen. Turning her around to face him, he tilted up her chin with a forefinger, gazed adoringly into her eyes, and fervently declared, "I love you!"

That did it. His words ignited a flame of indignation that blazed into fury. Her open palm delivered a powerful slap that snapped his head back and sideways, and left him nursing his face. Blinking and stunned, he opened his mouth, but once again, she cut him off.

"Get out!" she ordered, her eyes contemptuously raking him from head to toe.

"No," he said, crossing his arms and planting his feet in a stance of firm determination. "I refuse," he challenged her.

"You refuse?" she hissed.

"I refuse," he staunchly repeated, and sat down once more.

Sheila felt like slapping him again but instead decided to put an end to this farce once and for all. Without a word, she walked out of the room.

Diego remained seated. No matter how long it took, he would wait until she returned. He didn't have to wait long. Sheila came marching back into the room almost immediately. She flung a newspaper down onto the coffee table in front of him. She was glad she hadn't disposed of it, although she'd told herself countless times that the sooner she did, the sooner she could rid herself of the myth of Diego.

She jabbed at an article at the bottom of the page and challenged him, "Now deny that!"

It took him a while to get to the part that she intended him to read but at last, he did.

"So, this is the source of the trouble. Sheila, the article refers to my brother, José, not to me."

"That's easy enough for you to say. The groom's name is not mentioned in the article," she asserted.

"Exactly," he rejoined. While she thought this over, he said, "When I refused to reconcile with the woman called Rosa Galán, my father used his heart condition to try to get what he wanted, but by then, I knew he was in no danger of collapsing a second time. So, I informed him that I would no longer submit to emotional blackmail. My brother, José, has always been attracted to Rosa – to Elena. When I approached him about marrying her, he didn't hesitate to agree to replace me as the groom. She happily accepted him and, as they say, the rest is history."

When Sheila said nothing, Diego drew out a packet of photos from the inner pocket of his jacket. "Look, look at these!" he said.

The pictures showed a younger, taller and thinner man facing a stunning bride at the altar. Handing over a ring in the role of best man stood Diego, wearing a look of total satisfaction.

At last, Sheila was convinced. Such a weight lifted from her heart that, for a moment, she could only stare at the wedding pictures. When she finally did speak, her voice rose barely above a contrite whisper. "I'm sorry, Diego. I really hurt you, didn't I, darling?"

"Hurt me?" he said, gingerly touching his face where her palm print was still visible. "Lady, my face is still tingling. Your arm is fully functional, I see. But I will forgive you on two conditions."

"What are they?" Sheila asked.

"First, you must kiss it until it feels better."

After three kisses on the reddened area, he declared that it felt much better.

Giggling, she asked what the second condition was.

"Call me *darling* again. I love the sound of it."

"Darling," she softly complied.

"You *do* love me," he stated, tilting her chin up to gauge her expression.

"Yes, Diego, although I fought it in the beginning."

"Because of the engagement?" he asked.

"Yes. Then, when the news came out that you – I assumed it was you – that you had married Rosa, I mean Elena, I was devastated. I even wondered if your professed faith in Christ was genuine."

"It is genuine. *I* am genuine."

"I realize that now," Sheila said. "But Diego, between my skirting the embassy rules – until that night in the field –"

She broke off, swallowed hard and only continued when he said, "Courage!"

"Between my skirting the rules and the target on your back, it's a wonder that either of us made it out of Colombia alive."

"There was no target on my back," Diego coolly informed her.

"There – there wasn't? The embassy warned me off associating with you because of possible danger."

"Danger of my being kidnapped – or worse – for ransom?"

"Yes."

"That was highly unlikely because my family is not rich. Oh, our name has carried prestige for some generations and we have always been financially comfortable, obviously so, but – as I discovered after my father's death, we no longer were. The family business was on the brink of bankruptcy. My father saw Galán-Garza, or the man he *thought* was Galán-Garza, as his solution."

"Then, where was the danger?"

"There was none – or very little. You see, I was granted a kind of – amnesty, if you will, from the anti-government groups."

"Amnesty? Diego, are you saying that you had connections to M-19 and FARC?" Sheila asked in astonishment.

"Yes, but not in the way you are thinking. You remember the night of the confrontation with Davis."

"Oh, Diego, I wish I could forget it!"

"You will recall that I was so nervous, I could hardly steady the gun."

Sheila nodded, then concluded, "So, you're *not* a terrorist."

"Of course not!"

"Or a sympathizer or collaborator?"

"Definitely not."

"Then how did you get involved --?"

"I will try to make a long story short, as they say. A few years ago, I was visiting my maternal grandmother in Calí —"

"Calí, in Valle de Cauca, where the Colombian Army and FARC are fighting? Diego, that area is off-limits to embassy personnel!"

"I know. As I was saying, I was visiting my grandmother. She has since passed away. On the second day of my visit, I was — sought out and escorted to the battle field and — compelled to treat casualties among the FARC combatants. Among those that I was able to save were the head of the squadron and his two brothers."

"So, they befriended you?"

"*Befriended* is not a word to be associated with such men. Let us just say that the squadron leader conscripted my medical skills but, noting my abhorrence to violence, he assured me that I, my family, and the clinic would be exempt from any —

consequences *if* I agreed to cooperate. FARC was in dire need of doctors. So was M-19. Eventually, they too found that my services suited their purposes. They offered me the same deal. By the way, *Juan* was merely a driver, an M-19 *nobody*."

"So, the prospect of your family's wealth for ransom was never a factor?"

"Never. Both groups knew full well that there were much better prospects for ransom elsewhere. I doubt that even my medical skills could have restrained either FARC or M-19 if money had been an issue."

"I don't understand how you found the time to practice at the clinic and keep your part of those deals."

"I seldom did. They recruited Dr. Herrera, a sympathizer and MD at Palermo, as a go-between to watch me closely. I was never contacted directly. Herrera and I rotated. Fortunately, when I explained the situation to our clinic's director, he granted me a leave of absence whenever I requested it. The leaders of FARC and M-19 also had a personal interest in my going to Armero and Chiva-Chiva. Several of their relatives were victims. Few survived, by the way."

"And now –?"

"Now that José has married Rosa – Elena, the problem of safety is *his* and Carlos's, who will someday join the company. Once again, the business is solvent. You see, shortly before the assassinations -- immediately after the wedding -- a considerable sum was deposited into the company's account as a part of the marriage agreement."

Diego cleared his throat and went down on one knee.

"Speaking of marriage, I cannot imagine anyone else as my wife. So, Sheila Marie Dunbar, will you do me the honor --?"

"Yes, Diego!" Sheila cried, throwing her arms around his neck and receiving a kiss that left her breathless.

When she abruptly pulled away from him, he whispered, "Come back into my arms," then "Sheila, what is it?"

"You said – you wrote to me about breaking the engagement."

"Yes, I did. I wrote six letters to you."

"Six?" she said with wide eyes. "I received only two. I wonder –"

They suddenly became aware of her mother standing in the doorway of the den. Diego released her, and they faced her mother together with the announcement that they were going to get married.

"I heard. Where's the ring?" she asked, looking from one to the other with suspicion.

"Sheila will choose it. And, with time, I hope I may gain your approval, Mrs. Dunbar," Diego stated. When Dorothy remained silent, he added, "And now, I must go."

"Where are you staying?" Sheila asked.

"At a hotel near the airport," he replied. "May I use your telephone to call a taxi, Mrs. Dunbar?"

"Sure," the older woman answered stiffly, her presence hampering any further privacy between the two.

After calling a taxi, Diego sat in the den, holding Sheila's hand until the taxi driver honked his horn. With a quick kiss on Sheila's hand and a bow of the head to Dorothy, he promised to call Sheila the next day, then hurried outside.

"Who was that man?" Kevin's voice seemed to come from a long distance.

"Later, honey. We'll talk later," Sheila said.

"Sheila, please don't tell me that Latino is divorcing his wife to marry you," Dorothy commented. "Don't look at me like that. It was news all over the world for a week – 'an engagement, a wedding, a funeral' – don't be naïve."

When Sheila explained that Diego's brother was actually the man who married the woman posing as the cartel boss's daughter, her mother shook her head in astonishment, then returned to the subject of Diego himself.

"Tell me one thing," she said. "Were Black men so scarce in Bogotá that you had to take whatever you could get?"

"They weren't scarce, Mama, but as for Diego, I'd appreciate his not being placed in the category of whatever I could get."

"You do have a point. It could be worse. He certainly doesn't look penniless."

"I'm not marrying Diego for his money. He's the kind of man any woman would be proud to marry."

"Not any *Black* woman. Some of us haven't forgotten where we came from."

"What are you getting at?" Sheila asked, a slow, dull ache starting in her head.

"I'm talking about almost four hundred years of Black folks struggling to survive as a race in this country. Now you want to tie yourself to this ... this Diego. Wake up, girl! He's practically White! He'll make you forget your roots if he hasn't already."

"Mama, he hasn't, and he won't."

"Well, I hope there'll be no more mysteries in this saga. Enough is enough," she concluded as they all prepared for dinner.

Yet one final mystery remained in what Dorothy termed the "saga" – that of the other four letters that Diego had written to Sheila. The mystery of the missing letters would nag Sheila and Diego for a month until Dorothy, apparently too ashamed to face her daughter, left the thin stack on Sheila's dresser while she was at work. She chose a floral blank card and envelope, wrote a message inside, addressed it to "My dear daughter" and placed it on top of the stack. The message read, "I wanted to protect you and Kevin. I'm sorry. Please forgive me. Love, Mama."

When Sheila read it, she rushed into the kitchen, grabbed her mother from behind as Dorothy stood at the kitchen sink, and held on tight. "Oh, Mama!" she sobbed, "It's all right. Of course, I forgive you!"

CHAPTER 33

Sheila and Diego were married at Shiloh Missionary Baptist Church by Pastor Maynard in early October, 1988. Despite her preference for a Black son-in-law (specifically Matthew Stone, the MD), Dorothy attended the ceremony and even managed to maintain a pleasant façade throughout the reception. She noticed that Kevin had taken quite a liking to the Colombian doctor. He seemed to have a way with children – and, apparently, women too, as she herself was gradually warming up to his ways. He was as courteous as anybody could be and as downright friendly as Rags, the puppy which was growing by leaps and bounds. She had to admit that despite her disappointment in Sheila's decision to marry the man, she could find no fault in him except the fact that he was a bit of a workaholic. Since establishing his medical credentials in the States and being hired at a research laboratory, he hadn't even taken Sheila on a proper honeymoon. It had been three months, and Diego, on most days, worked from sunrise to sunset, with the exception of Sundays. It appeared that he was focusing more and more on pediatric oncology. Meanwhile, Sheila had reapplied and been accepted into the Master's program at Howard University but later dropped out. Maybe she was learning that a woman just couldn't have it all, not at the same time. Dorothy didn't care what the women's libbers said; there had to be balance somewhere, which meant something had to give!

As for her own life, Dorothy had begun to keenly feel the absence of her daughter and grandson when they'd moved out. She had gotten so accustomed to having them in the house that she looked forward to their visits, especially Kevin's, more than ever. She did keep busy with her church sewing circle and volunteered at a local pantry, but she still missed having them around every day.

Nevertheless, it looked as if Dorothy's lonely days would soon be over when the widowed Mr. Atkinson came calling daily. He invited her to concerts, dinners, picnics, ballgames, art galleries, museums, and any other events he could think of. Oh, the man was a veritable lightning rod, Dorothy concluded. Who would have thought that at nearly sixty, she'd be out and about so much and having the time of her life? And he was just as active at church as she was. Could this be the start of a second chance at love for her? Despite her happiness, she told herself that she mustn't get carried away. After all, they hadn't known each other very long. But, Drew – Andrew, that is – had already introduced her to his son, daughter-in-law, and three grandchildren, a girl and two boys. Her emotions were like a tangled ball of yarn.

Sheila and Diego were quick to notice the positive change in Dorothy's demeanor, and they were glad that Kevin had adopted her beau as a surrogate grandpa. Still, they looked forward to the day when they could have a real honeymoon. That quick trip to Bogotá after the wedding had been anything but happy. Diego's stepmother, Carmenza, in mourning for her husband and dressed totally in black, was in no mood to entertain a new daughter-in-law. Diego's siblings, Carlos and Conchita, had been very welcoming; but José and Elena, perhaps understandably, were cool toward the newlyweds as they all dined at a local restaurant. Sheila and Diego cut short their visit with his family and made a quick detour to Cartagena for three days before flying back to the States.

****

January 9, 1989

Silver Spring, Maryland

Dear Pat and Liz,

Yes, it's true. Diego and I are married and living in Maryland. To my great relief, it was his brother José who married Elena Pacheco (alias Rosa Galán), but how sad that Fabio Santos lost his life because he didn't know who Guzman really was!

My mother has found happiness with Andrew Atkinson, a retired and widowed Air Force officer who settled in the DC area about a year and a half ago. They're living in northeast DC in a rowhouse that he bought before they met. (The one I grew up in provides them some rental income.) They honeymooned in Paris of all places!

So, you're going to Switzerland. I was there during my final undergrad year on a whirlwind tour of Europe. It's beautiful — and peaceful.

Pat, we must take the bitter with the sweet in this life. My condolences on the loss of your Uncle Max. Dementia is a cruel disease. We can only donate and pray for a cure soon. You can take comfort knowing that he was a believer and is now with our Lord.

Well, the Master warned His disciples of coming tribulations, and I believe that applies to us today too. My little Kevin (who's not so little anymore) has just been diagnosed with diabetes, but he hasn't missed a beat. As long as we keep him on a proper diet, a good physical regimen, and insulin, he'll be fine. He wants to become an MD someday, like his new dad. I'll be one proud mom if he follows through. As for Diego, he's involved in pediatric oncology research. The man is a workaholic, but I can't complain. He gives 100 percent when he's at home.

We hope to have a real honeymoon on our first anniversary. (Kevin will stay with Mama and Andrew.) Just imagine a whole month on Santa Marta Island! I may even learn to swim.

Bogotá taught us some valuable lessons, one being that God is faithful. Look at what he brought us through!

Enough. I must prepare dinner. That sweet husband of mine will be home soon, and so far, diabetes hasn't diminished Kevin's appetite at all.

Congratulations on your upcoming assignment to Bern! Keep in touch.

In His love,

Sheila

****

May 6, 1989

Bern, Switzerland

Dear Sheila,

It's been quite a while since we've been in touch, but that's life in the Foreign Service for you — at least for me since you're now in the State Department's Civil Service. I'm glad that being back home hasn't quenched your thirst for travel. You know that Liz and I have the welcome mat out anytime you and yours want to visit.

So, you didn't lose your employment because of your marriage to Dr. Santos. It seems his reputation at the Clínica Palermo and with Doctors Without Borders far exceeded the poor judgment of his late father.

We've been here in Bern since early March, and you won't believe our new quarters! It's a spacious apartment in a castle outside the city. The commute isn't bad. Some would say it's worth it to live in a thirteenth-century castle. It's beautiful at night with the turrets lit up. All that cream-colored stone magically turns gold (unless that's just the special lighting). We were elated when they told us where we'd be living, but a long winter revealed why they used to cover the walls in huge tapestries and the floors in thick rugs. *B-r-r-r!*

Bern is just the assignment we need. A much slower pace, picturesque, and with a manageable workload. Liz and I have already toured several cantons and are enjoying the cheese (think fondue) and the chocolate (second to none). I could go on and on, but you get my drift.

Being at headquarters, you've probably heard the latest news, but just in case you haven't kept up with our staff from Colombia, here goes.

The biggest news is that Ambassador Váldez got assigned to Athens – and he didn't go alone. Remember the retired Consular Officer on temporary duty? It seems they were old friends who go way back, so old acquaintances were renewed, and the confirmed bachelor is a bachelor no more. He and the widow Morgan tied the knot upon completion of his tour of duty in Bogotá and are probably dancing to Greek bouzouki music every night.

Hold on to your hat! Christy is no longer in the Foreign Service! We all got a shock six months after she arrived in Rome when word came down that she was marrying some Italian count. It seems his family hails from Florence but also has an estate somewhere in the Tuscan hills where the vineyards are plentiful and, thus, the wine flows freely. Next week, we're told, she'll be Contessa Christy, wife of Count Cesare Casanova. Let's hope his surname isn't indicative of his character. What is it about Bogotá – some lovebug biting staff at random?

Please congratulate your mother for us. So, she married Mr. Atkinson, the neighbor, and they honeymooned in Paris. We can't blame the Bogotá lovebug for that, can we?

More news – and equally as significant: Mr. Landers is doing well and is expected to be back on the foreign circuit soon because of the fairly early diagnosis and removal of those moles. He can thank your husband and Portia for overcoming his aversion to conventional medicine.

Rod Radcliff retired (and high time, if I may say so), opting out of a final plum post: Nassau.

Brad Davis was replaced in the RSO by Agent Dan Chu, whose last post was Beijing. Sam Sheridan, the rookie, is going to Guatemala City. Witt Jones has extended in Bogotá for an additional year. Ty Collier of DEA is headed to Quito.

As for my former sidekicks, Walter Stanwyk has just gotten his orders for Oaugadougou, Burkina Faso. Calvin Brenner is happily headed to London. He used to say, "No cats, no Calvin," because of the six-month quarantine requirement for animals at some posts, but go figure; his sister in Chicago has agreed to care for Muffin and Misty, so off he goes. What do you want to bet he'll be cozying up to the guard detail at Buckingham Palace just to get a glimpse of the Queen?

Lest I forget, Deputy Chief of Mission Sandra Charlemagne is being assigned to Tel Aviv. You know there's talk of moving our embassy in Israel to Jerusalem. I think that was the reason for listing it as her number one choice. However, I don't think she should hold her breath. How long have we been hearing that same rumor? I could be wrong, but I think it will be a while before there's a US Embassy in Jerusalem.

As for the rest of our direct-hire staff, Thompson, Brandt, Paxton, Temple, and Sweetwater are still in Bogotá, awaiting word of their next assignments. Until then, may God and the RSO protect them all!

Guess you heard about the Colombian Supreme Court tossing out our extradition treaty with Colombia not long after you left. Looks like the guerillas will soon be negotiating with the current regime if they haven't already started.

Last, but certainly not least, Liz and I found a great church family here. It's St. Ursula's Anglican Church, within a couple of blocks' walking distance from the embassy. We attend regularly and are slowly but surely growing in His grace. And to think our true Christian journey began at the Bogotá Baptist Chapel! Liz and I are grateful, my friend. The Gospel is good news indeed!

Give our best to Diego, Kevin and the Atkinsons. Keep looking up!

Pat and Liz

p.s. Cynthia Nelson is on extended leave. I didn't know she was married, but I hear she has a sick husband in New Mexico who needs her.

CHAPTER 34

October, 1989

Island of Santa Marta, Colombia

I t had been three weeks since Diego and Sheila arrived on the island of Santa Marta, and what a honeymoon it had been so far! They'd begun at a frenetic pace as Sheila became enthralled with her swimming lessons, and Diego refreshed his scuba diving and guitar-playing skills. Then, there were the wonderful tropical fruits, seafood, and produce.

On this particular evening, they were sipping a pineapple-coconut smoothie as they snuggled on a loveseat and gazed at the stars from the terrace of their tiny rented bungalow.

"Anyone who says there is no God has never seen this place," Sheila remarked.

"I totally agree," Diego responded, then added, "Psalms 14:1 says such a person is a fool. Imagine a world without God!"

They fell silent, each pondering the idea. It was Diego who broke the silence. "Sheila, while you were at your lesson this morning, I called my friend Lorenzo in Bogotá."

"Lorenzo. Oh yes, I remember him and his frosty 'Welcome.' He kept calling me *Morena* and never once said my name."

Diego winced. "I know. There was no excuse for his behavior, and I told him so. His prejudice toward you and your mother's attitude toward me have been proverbial thorns in my flesh."

"But my mother's opinion of you has changed. To know you is to love you."

"You angel," he whispered, pressing his lips to her hair.

"So, what's the latest from Lorenzo?"

"He and Cecilia, his wife, have reconciled and are expecting their first child in seven months."

"That's wonderful news. Diego, why the long face? Aren't you happy for them?"

"Yes, of course, but –"

"But?"

"I confess that I am envious. Sheila, we have been trying for a year now and –"

"No baby on the way yet, but it's been fun trying, hasn't it?" Sheila said with a grin and a light kiss on the tip of his nose.

"Yes," he admitted. "I cannot complain. Our nights have been—"

"Blissful," Sheila broke in.

"Pure ecstasy. *Te adoro*," Diego said, encircling her with his arms.

"You adore me? Well, that's enough for me. Darling, don't worry. Our time will come."

He said nothing, but his furrowed brow gave Sheila a jolt of concern. "Diego, there's something you're not telling me. What is it?"

"Before we left, I was tested – to determine whether or not I am sterile. I suspected that I might be. You see, many years ago, I was exposed to rubella."

"German measles?"

He nodded. "The lab called yesterday."

"And?"

"It is conclusive."

"So?"

"Sheila, I am so very sorry. I should have told you of the possibility *before* we married, but I was afraid of losing you. Then I tried to deny that it could happen to me, *willed* it not to happen –"

"Sh!" she said. "It's all right, Diego."

"All right?" he repeated in a shocked tone. "You – you are not feeling disappointed, betrayed?"

"Of course not. I'm disappointed, but only for you. I know how much you wanted children. As much as I wanted to give you a child, I have no pleasant memories of pregnancy. I was on bed rest for the last three of the nine months, my blood pressure went up dangerously high, the labor was long and hard, and Kevin was born by Cesarean section."

"So, you would not … reconsider the marriage?" he asked, a note of caution in his voice.

"Divorce? Not because of that, silly."

"Then, for some other reason you might leave me?"

"Leave you? Uhm, let me think. I guess I'd have no choice if there were abuse, or you became a *mujeriego*," she teased, a finger on her chin.

"Abuse? Womanizing? Sheila, you know me better than that. I took a vow. I love you!"

Sheila laughed. "I know. You've told me at least a hundred times."

"And I will tell you a hundred times more if it will convince you," Diego declared.

"No need. I'm convinced. I love you too, and I trust you. I'm not going anywhere."

"Neither am I – ever," Diego intoned, drawing her close for a lingering kiss.

Into this delightful moment burst a shout of panic. "Dr. Santos, come quickly!"

It was the desperate plea of the resort's head groundskeeper that brought about the traumatic events of that night. Luis Quintana's wife was in labor, and there wasn't enough time to get her to a hospital. Diego joined the emergency medical technician on duty in valiant efforts to safely deliver the twins. Sadly, María Carmen, the twenty-eight-year-old mother, did not survive. The thirty-year-old father was devastated by her death but became inconsolable when he learned of the health conditions of his newborn children. His daughter, Luz-Clara, emerged with Down syndrome. The baby boy, Juan Miguel, was born with empty eye sockets – totally blind.

Naturally, the resort allowed Luis time off to grieve and handle his affairs; however, just seven days after his wife's death, he too was gone. Rumors flew. One fact was certain. He had drowned.

"But how?" his older sister, María Teresa, asked. "He was a strong swimmer."

A supposed eyewitness reported that Luis had simply walked into the water farther and farther out until his head disappeared beneath the waves. Another swore that Luis had been far out to sea when a gigantic wave struck him and swept him away. Wherever the truth lay, it was up to the young doctor to note the causes of death for both wife and husband, and to sign certificates of death. The cause of María Carmen's death was never in doubt; however, in Luis's case, Diego rejected all speculation and simply noted that he had drowned.

Both families of the couple were extensive, but he was told that none had the resources to care for two infants who would require specialized medical care into adulthood. The tragedy hit Diego hard. He wept with the families and lost his appetite. That's when Sheila asked, just a day before they were to leave for the States, "Couldn't we take them, Diego?"

That marked the beginning of their journey together on a new parenting adventure. They extended their stay by another week to start the legal adoption process.

CHAPTER 35

Six years later, Sheila and Diego were back on the island of Santa Marta in another rented bungalow. On a cloudless, sunny day, they once again relaxed on a loveseat and luxuriated in the sounds of tropical birdsong and crashing waves while cool Caribbean breezes caressed their faces.

"Who could have fathomed that we would be here again under such different circumstances?" Diego remarked.

"Not I," Sheila said, then asked, "Regrets?"

"None. We have so much to be grateful for – each other, our children. You are studying again, and I have my work."

"In that order?"

"Yes, Sheila. It was your idea that we adopt the babies. Bringing them back here periodically to get to know their relatives was another good idea of yours. They realize we are doing what is best for the little ones. God turned the sterility that I thought of as a curse into a blessing."

"Speaking of blessings, did you notice how excited Luz-Clara was while watching the activity in the birdbath the other day?"

"I did. I thought we might have to gag her and close the curtain!" Diego said with a chuckle.

Sheila nodded.

"She squealed so loudly that Kevin dropped the phone, and Mama, on the other end, asked what was happening. But when Juan Miguel began strumming his guitar, she calmed down."

"His instructor is impressed by his skills. He says Juan Miguel is showing great promise for a six-year-old."

"Who knows?" Sheila remarked. "We may be the parents of another Andrés Segovia someday."

"Let us not get carried away, *querida*! He has a long way to go, but being blind has not hindered him."

"If anything, it seems to have enhanced his musical ability. They say that when one sense is lacking, another compensates."

"True. Well, I am proud of all our children."

"They've brought us so much joy, haven't they?" Sheila noted.

"Much joy but also a few tears. It is good to have this vacation just for the two of us," Diego commented.

"Oh, that reminds me. We'd better call home. Luz-Clara can be a handful at times, and God help us all when Kevin gets his regular driver's license!"

"In a few more years," Diego soothed.

When they returned to the front deck, Sheila settled back against the warmth of Diego's chest and said, "Since all's well at home, we can relax."

"Not quite," he soberly remarked.

She sat up to gaze into his face. "What's wrong, darling? Is your stomach acting up again? I think you ate too much shrimp at lunch."

"No, *vida mía*. My stomach is fine. This time, it is my heart."

"Diego!" Sheila gasped, leaping to her feet.

"It is racing – with passion!" he cried, pulling her onto his knees and kissing her with abandon.

As he released her, she exclaimed, "Don't *ever* do that again. You almost scared me to death!"

"My sincerest apologies, *señora,*" he intoned dramatically.

"Oh, you clown!" she said, swatting his arm before submitting to another kiss.

Some minutes later, they were reflecting on their years together thus far.

"Life with you has been beautiful – more than I ever dared hope for on this earth."

"Diego, you romantic! You can say that despite all we've been through?"

"*Because* of all we've been through and are still going through."

Sheila nodded. "God has been faithful," she said.

"Yes. He promised the children of Israel that He would never leave or forsake them, and we have rested on that same promise, especially when our faith was tested."

"And our love was under fire, but we put our trust in God, and He's been with us every step of the way, guiding us and keeping us strong."

"Sheila, *mi amor*, through Him, we are more than conquerors."

There was no further need for words. With their fingers entwined, they sat quietly, the marvelous sights and sounds of nature stirring their senses. A peace surpassing human understanding enveloped them, and the profound love in their eyes spoke volumes.

CHAPTER 36

April, 2014

Silver Spring, Maryland

The late afternoon sunlight was gradually waning. A lazy breeze swept over the brick patio where Sheila and Diego sat beneath a candy-striped umbrella, sipping coffee and snacking on lemon squares from a local bakery.

Sheila reached out to smooth back a stray curl off Diego's forehead. At the same time, he gently wiped her crumb-covered mouth with a paper napkin - gestures done countless times before with tender affection, but now with little to no thought.

Normally, they would be laughing and talking, reveling in being able to spend more time together now that they were empty nesters while, at the same time, excitedly anticipating the birth of their first grandchild. (Kevin's wife, Caroline, was expecting.) They would also be marveling at the fact that they had been able to purchase this lovely stone cottage at such a great price — a cottage that suited their decision to downsize.

The topic usually would turn to some present-day event: mass shootings, human and man-made disasters, disputes within church and government, rapidly changing technologies, the looming specter of an epidemic or – God forbid - a pandemic, etc. However, they seldom worried. They had prepared for the future, but always tried to live in the moment with generosity and gratitude for their many blessings. Their consciences were clear, their love for each other stronger than ever. Yet, getting here had not been easy. They had had to draw deeply from the well of their faith in God and their mutual support. A rare disagreement was usually settled by searching the scriptures. Today, however, was not a day for one of their spirited discussions. Had it not been for the sounds from their garden, the silence would have been overwhelming.

A profusion of flowering plants spilled from huge, glazed cobalt-blue pots occupying a third of the patio. The back yard was packed with a variety of budding trees and shrubs, flitting butterflies, buzzing bees, and birds calling, chirping and warbling. Here and there, among winding paths, stood colorful birdbaths, fountains, small statues, shaded benches, and more large potted plants. A cloudless sky smiled down on the entire garden, a potential refuge exuding beauty, peace and charm, but the couple hardly noticed their idyllic surroundings. For this was not an idyllic day. Their hearts were heavy with grief.

"I cannot believe she is gone!" Diego brokenly exclaimed with shimmering eyes. "I wish I could have done more!" His despondency was evident as he hung his head.

"It was quick, wasn't it?" Sheila remarked, covering his hands with both of hers. "But, Diego, you mustn't blame yourself. Heart disease is not uncommon in Down syndrome cases. As a physician, you know that better than most. You did all you humanly could. You realize that, don't you?"

"Yes, but —"

Placing a gentle finger on his lips, Sheila continued, "We knew when we adopted Luz-Clara that her health issues might take her from us — early."

"*Too* early," Diego said.

"It was God's timing, not ours."

Diego nodded and said, "You are right, *mi amor*. 'The Lord has given, and the Lord has taken away'."

"Blessed be the name of the Lord," Sheila said, finishing the quote of Job 1:21.

With quiet resignation, Diego remarked, "Tomorrow will be a very difficult day."

"Funerals usually are, but He will give us the strength to get through it."

"He always has," Diego agreed. "I remember when…"

They began talking about the trials their family had gone through over the years, including the nightmares triggered by post-traumatic stress as a result of their own experiences in Colombia. Counseling, meditation, and prayer had helped them to deal with it all and eventually emerge whole.

Then there had been the challenges their children had faced. Luz-Clara became the target of cruel bullying although her innocent, trusting nature often did not recognize it as such. Kevin had a couple of scares as a diabetic — one particularly horrifying when he was detained and kept in the county jail — a case of mistaken identity — without access to his insulin before being released one night later. Juan Miguel's guitar skills declined while he was studying Braille and training with a service dog.

To help their children cope with their issues, Sheila came up with the idea of plastic cards engraved with Bible verses, specifically chosen for each child's need and easily placed in wallets or a coin purse. For Luz-Clara, they selected Psalm 139:14, "I will praise You, for I am fearfully and wonderfully made." For Kevin, they chose a portion of Proverbs 17:22, "A merry heart does good like medicine." Juan Miguel's card in Braille quoted Matthew 5:8, "Blessed are the pure in heart. For they shall see God." These "reminders" proved helpful in times of flagging faith.

A severe injury at Colombia's famous annual cycling event had left Diego with a permanent limp. Sheila was treated for second-stage breast cancer and had been in remission for the past ten years. Sheila's mother and stepfather had been killed by a drunk driver in the wrong lane of an interstate highway. Diego's stepmother never recovered from her husband's assassination; she ended her own life with an overdose of sleeping pills. Through it all, their church family had rallied behind them, but it was their shared faith that sustained them as they prayed together and searched the scriptures for guidance and comfort.

Now, taking a deep breath of the fresh evening air, Diego said, "*We* would do well to remember that He has never forsaken us."

"And He never will," Sheila concluded.

****

As funerals go, Luz-Clara's was brief – an hour and a half. In the first two pews, reserved for the family, sat Diego, Sheila, Dr. Kevin Horne and wife Caroline, and Juan Miguel with his fiancée, Dora Lynn. Diego's sister Concepción (now a medical doctor) sat beside her husband, Javier Contreras, also a physician. Also present were Maria Teresa, the twins' aunt from Santa Marta, and Andrew's son, daughter-in-law and three grandchildren. Pat and Liz Carmichael were there to pay their final respects as were Mrs. Graham, Luz-Clara's high school teacher, several former classmates, and many church members as well as people from the community. To Sheila and Diego's surprise, Pastor Pittman, formerly of the Bogotá Baptist Chapel, put in a surprise appearance. Now retired and visibly frail, he sat in a wheelchair in the pulpit beside Pastor Maynard of Shiloh Missionary Baptist Church.

A recital of "The Lord's Prayer" preceded a reading of the 23rd Psalm. A congregational hymn, "I'll Fly Away" was followed by the moving gospel rendition of "Move on Up a Little Higher" (sung Mahalia Jackson-style by a hefty, full-throated choir member). Kevin read the eulogy and presented a slide show which had everyone laughing and crying by turns as they focused on the life of a young woman who never lost her child-like faith and joy in simple things. Pastor Maynard's thirty-minute sermon was based on I Corinthians 15 and ended with "Death is swallowed up in victory!"

A second surprise was the song written and performed by Dora, who was accompanied by a pianist and cellist. Diego and Sheila tightly clasped their hands, drawing solace from the lyrics:

> *Beyond all time and space*
>
> *There is a better place*

Promised to all who will believe.

No more pain, no more sorrow

In that home of tomorrow

No more tears

For He'll wipe them all away

No more death, no more night

For the Son will be our Light

*And our song shall ever be of highest praise! **

Fittingly, the service ended with the doxology and Luz-Clara's favorite "Jesus Loves the Little Children" as everyone filed out of the sanctuary. On that sunny afternoon, Luz-Clara would be laid to rest near her Grandma Dottie and Grandpa Drew.

*Excerpt from "A Better Place," original lyrics and music by author.

EPILOGUE

One year later:

"Darling, I'm so happy, I could cry!" Sheila exclaimed.

They were in the bedroom of their cottage, changing into comfortable clothes after the wedding ceremony and reception of their son, Juan Miguel, and his bride, Dora Lynn.

Diego coolly remarked, "*Querida*, I wonder if you have any tears left. I thought I would have to request a janitor to mop them up at the church."

"Don't tell me *you* didn't shed a tear or two," Sheila huffed.

"Precisely. A tear or two. Not a bucket," Diego said with a grin.

"You're exaggerating, but I don't care. Nothing's going to rain on my parade — not today. Isn't it wonderful that Juan Miguel found a wife who shares his passion for music *and* his love for the Lord?"

"Indeed," Diego agreed. "It is even more wonderful that they can minister together through their music. They are booked beyond this year."

"Oh, I do wish they didn't have to travel so much."

"But their life's work requires it — at least for now."

"You're right. Theirs is a match made in heaven."

"So was ours," Diego said with an adoring sideways glance.

"Oh, yes! Heaven-sent and heaven on earth!" Sheila said, dramatically sighing, then adding, "Seriously, our marriage has been tested in more ways than one. I suppose all marriages are."

"And some do not survive. Ours has not only survived but thrived."

"Despite the testing," Sheila commented.

"*Because* of the testing. Has not love itself – *His* love – been our refiner over these many years?"

"The Bible speaks of a refining fire."

"Yes. As fire that burns away the impurities in gold and silver, the fire of His love has refined – burned away – the threats to our marriage."

"What threats?" Sheila teased with a gasp of mock horror.

"No more drama, Sheila! The immediate one was the nightmares. We were fighting a common enemy – and won. But perhaps the steepest hill we had to climb was that of forgiveness."

"You're talking about that woman who killed Mama and Drew. She was so drunk, it was two days before they could question her. Driving on a revoked license!" Sheila said, shaking her head.

"In the end, it was cirrhosis of the liver that almost had the final word."

"Almost? Oh, I know what you mean. Our forgiving her gave her the peace she never found in a bottle."

"Yes, and we found peace in knowing that we had done what was right."

"I wish we could forget all that," Sheila said.

"As do I, but we *must* remember, or be reminded when we least expect it."

"Spoken like a *true* sage."

"Then there was my jealousy. I was jealous of the time you spent with others – your mother, even our children. I wanted you *all* to myself, Sheila. That was jealousy brought on by selfishness."

"I plead guilty to both. You were very devoted to your work and I began to resent those extra hours at work, away from me – until we talked it out and resolved it."

"Fear," Diego continued.

"Of what?" Sheila asked.

"Losing you. As much as I came to love your mother – and her cooking – I was afraid she might turn you against me."

"Didn't I tell you that her attitude changed early on in our marriage? I was an only child. She came to love you like a son."

"I realized that – later."

"Well, I too had to deal with my fear. Fear of not pleasing you."

"You are joking, no?"

"No, I'm not. Diego, you placed me on a pedestal. I knew I couldn't live up to all that adulation. I was afraid that I would fail you and you'd end up disappointed in me, even regret –"

"Never!" he exclaimed. "Never have I been disappointed in you or regretted marrying you."

"I know that now, but back then —"

"Back then, we both had our — insecurities," Diego said. "Which brings me to the biggest of all: pride."

"That *is* big," Sheila said, quoting Proverbs 16:18. "Pride goes before destruction. And a haughty spirit before a fall."

"Pride, most of all, in my work. And yet, I have never found a cure for even one childhood cancer. I have made a lot of progress in treatments, but never succeeded in finding a cure. Failure has certainly humbled me."

"We only fail when we give up, and you never have. You've been a fantastic husband and father. With Kevin's aversion to flies, he never would have gone into forensic medicine if you hadn't sparked his interest by explaining the importance of insects in medical investigations."

"A field that I personally would not have chosen. I am convinced that medical examiners are the undervalued ones, working so much behind-the-scenes as they do. Pride makes fools of many doctors."

 "But there's a good kind of pride. I'm proud to be your wife."

"And I am so proud that you *are*. Your loyalty, patience, and kindness, your beauty — "

"My beauty? Diego, I'm turning grey!"

"*We* are turning *silver*, and it is *most* becoming to us. Is it not?"

"If you say so," Sheila said with a shrug.

"That is another thing I admire about you — your modesty. And your eyes!" Diego went on. "Do you know that on that first day in the park, they captivated me? They *still* do."

"Diego, stop it!"

"It is true. But your skin. After all these years, it remains as smooth as rich, dark chocolate – a delight beneath my fingertips! As they say, 'The black will not crack'."

"Oh, is that what they say?" Sheila asked, one eyebrow raised in amusement.

"Ah! Your lips," Diego enthused, "I confess that I find them irresistible."

Sheila dimpled and leaned in against his chest.

"Do you know what I find most appealing about you?" she asked in a velvety voice.

"No. What?"

"Your way with words and –"

"Yes?"

"Your perfect eyesight," she replied matter-of-factly.

He burst out laughing. Shortly, his breathing settled. "My little comedian."

"Well, you started it. Remember that Santa Marta gag? Your heart 'racing with passion'?" Sheila mimicked.

"Fair enough. But, believe me when I say *thank you* for simply being you. I love you most for how you have stood beside me these twenty-seven years. It has meant the world to me."

"If I were a vain woman, I'd blush – if I could!" Sheila exclaimed. "No, Diego, it's only God's grace that has sustained us through all the ups and downs of our life together."

She stepped back and held him at arm's length as if to survey him with new eyes. "But I think our best days are ahead of us. What do *you* think?"

"I think the best days begin with the best moments, and we need not wait for tomorrow. Come back into my arms!" he whispered.

Sheila gladly obeyed, eagerly lifting her face for his kiss.

****

Later that afternoon, the two lovebirds retreated to their patio. Briefly, they bowed their heads to pray that Kevin and Caroline would be spared the heartache of a second miscarriage. They then sat back to relax and enjoy coffee, lemon squares, and Diego's guitar strumming.

"You should have played a tribute to Juan Miguel and Dora," Sheila said.

"You *know* how much I dislike performing before an audience. It was difficult enough serenading you at our last anniversary celebration. But tell me what you think of these lyrics," he said, handing her a sheet of paper.

"When did Dora –?"

"These are mine, penned especially for you."

Sheila sat back and relaxed as the words washed over her in a tranquil wave.

> *Love's refining fire*
>
> *Fulfill our hearts' desire*
>
> *Purify our souls*
>
> *Like silver and gold*
>
> *As your flames keep rising higher**

"Bravo!" Sheila softly applauded.

After Diego put his guitar aside, he extended his hand to help Sheila to her feet and planted his customary kiss on her hair. Then tucking her hand into the bend of his arm, he beckoned, *"Ven, mi amor." Come, my love.* Together, they set off on a stroll through their lovely garden.

THE END

*Excerpt from original song lyrics by author.

ACKNOWLEDGMENTS

My gratitude to Jason Collins, Publishing and Marketing Director, and Derrick Hogan, Fulfillment Officer, Citi of Books, for their patience and professionalism during this publishing journey. Further thanks to the editors, page design and book cover design teams.

I would be remiss if I failed to mention the awesome staff of the East Mountain/Tijeras branch of the Albuquerque-Bernalillo County Library system. Without their assistance and computer expertise, this book could not have been finalized. They are, namely, John Haggerty, Corey Bowen, Carmen Martinez, and Lynne Fothergill.

To the very talented Justin Jew and staff at Kim Jew Photography, you're the best! You make even a camera-shy lady shine.

Above all, a big "Thank you!" to my Lord and Savior, Jesus Christ; for it is He "who strengthens me."

LOVE'S REFINING FIRE

Synopsis

The love story of Sheila Dunbar, US Embassy office manager, and Diego Santos, a physician, unfolds in mid-1980's Bogotá, Colombia. The era and the nation are shaken by terrorism fomented by drug trafficking on an epidemic scale. In turn, a US-Colombian extradition treaty aims to combat and destroy that illicit trade.

In <u>Love Under Fire</u>, the predecessor to this book, the reader was given glimpses of embassy operations and the profiles of various characters, both inside and outside the US diplomatic community. <u>Love's Refining Fire</u> retains much of those elements but expands on them and adds more detail so that the reader gets a broader view of the circumstances surrounding the story. It also explores more deeply the essence of the theme: true love overcoming obstacles. Challenges abound and changes are inevitable, but through them all, God is faithful. Trusting in Him and each other, the two main characters, Sheila and Diego, are sustained, not merely for a season, but for a lifetime of seasons.

May those of us who have chosen to walk the narrow path of faith be encouraged by their story.

!Bendiciones! (Blessings!)

Dorothea